She _____ *the*

Recollections of his smile flashed through her memory like summer lightning. Memories of the hurt and confusion her decisions had caused stung like the sparks coming off a Fourth-of-July sparkler.

Her stomach flipped and her hands began to sweat.

Trace McCabe.

The reason Jennifer had stayed away from her hometown for eight years.

Then she turned, and his easy grin became a look of disbelief, shock—followed by a flash of anger.

Dangerous thoughts and emotions shook her. Her stomach jittered just as it used to when she was seventeen.

Perhaps her feelings hadn't been buried as deeply as she'd thought.

Dear Reader,

To me, September is the cruelest month. One minute it feels like just another glorious summer day. And then almost overnight the days become shorter and life just hits. It's no different for this month's heroes and heroines. Because they all get their own very special "September moment" when they discover a secret that will change their lives forever!

Judy Christenberry once again heads up this month with *The Texan's Tiny Dilemma* (#1782)—the next installment in her LONE STAR BRIDES miniseries. A handsome accountant must suddenly figure out how to factor love into the equation when a one-night stand results in twins. Seth Bryant gets his wake-up call when a very pregnant princess shows up on his doorstep in *Prince Baby* (#1783), which continues Susan Meier's BRYANT BABY BONANZA. Jill Limber assures us that *The Sheriff Wins a Wife* (#1784) in the continuing BLOSSOM COUNTY FAIR continuity, *but* how will this lawman react to the news that he's still married to a woman who left town eight years ago! Holly Jacobs rounds out the month with her next PERRY SQUARE: THE ROYAL INVASION! title. In *Once Upon a King* (#1785), baby seems to come before love and marriage for a future king.

And be sure to watch for more great romances next month when bestselling author Myrna Mackenzie launches our new SHAKESPEARE IN LOVE miniseries.

Happy reading,

Ann Leslie Tuttle
Associate Senior Editor

Please address questions and book requests to:
Silhouette Reader Service
U.S.: 3010 Walden Ave., P.O. Box 1325, Buffalo, NY 14269
Canadian: P.O. Box 609, Fort Erie, Ont. L2A 5X3

Robbie Hopson
Annette Davis
good
Pam

The *Sheriff* Wins a Wife

JILL LIMBER

SILHOUETTE Romance ®

Published by Silhouette Books

America's Publisher of Contemporary Romance

If you purchased this book without a cover you should be aware
that this book is stolen property. It was reported as "unsold and
destroyed" to the publisher, and neither the author nor the
publisher has received any payment for this "stripped book."

To Matthew and Zachary: my newest little heroes

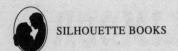 SILHOUETTE BOOKS

ISBN 0-373-19784-5

THE SHERIFF WINS A WIFE

Copyright © 2005 by Jill Limber

All rights reserved. Except for use in any review, the reproduction
or utilization of this work in whole or in part in any form by any
electronic, mechanical or other means, now known or hereafter
invented, including xerography, photocopying and recording, or in
any information storage or retrieval system, is forbidden without
the written permission of the editorial office, Silhouette Books,
233 Broadway, New York, NY 10279 U.S.A.

All characters in this book have no existence outside the imagination of
the author and have no relation whatsoever to anyone bearing the same
name or names. They are not even distantly inspired by any individual
known or unknown to the author, and all incidents are pure invention.

This edition published by arrangement with Harlequin Books S.A.

® and TM are trademarks of Harlequin Books S.A., used under license.
Trademarks indicated with ® are registered in the United States Patent
and Trademark Office, the Canadian Trade Marks Office and in other
countries.

Visit Silhouette Books at www.eHarlequin.com

Printed in U.S.A.

Books by Jill Limber

Silhouette Romance

The 15 lb. Matchmaker #1593
Captivating a Cowboy #1664
Daddy, He Wrote #1756
The Sheriff Wins a Wfe #1784

Silhouette Intimate Moments

Secrets of an Old Flame #1266

JILL LIMBER

lives in San Diego with her husband. Now that her children are grown, their two dogs keep her company while she sits at her computer writing stories. A native Californian, she enjoys the beach, loves to swim in the ocean, and for relaxation she daydreams and reads romances. You can learn more about Jill by visiting her Web site at www.JillLimber.com.

THE BLOSSOM BEE

The Buzz About Town
By: Harriet Hearsay

We've got the dirt…straight from the pigpen!

It seems Jennifer Williams, now of Dallas, is back in town and helping her niece with Petunia the pig. But don't you know, this girl is clueless about hogs and she nearly landed flat on her behind the first time in the pen. Surprise, surprise—guess who was there to pull her out of the muck and straight into his arms? Her old flame, Sheriff Trace McCabe! This columnist is definitely ready to watch the mud fly between these two!

Chapter One

Jennifer Williams tried to avoid breathing through her nose.

It had been eight years since she'd been to the Blossom County fair, and she'd forgotten how bad the smell of the animal barn could get during the heat of the day.

She'd never been involved in 4H in school. Her mother hadn't allowed her or her sister to participate. Ellen Williams had declared that no daughter of hers was going to lower herself to clean up after an animal. Jennifer had felt left out; all her friends had raised 4H animals. But now, standing beside the smelly pen that held her niece Kelly's 4H entry, Jennifer thought perhaps her mother had had a point.

Petunia the pig was large, pink and cranky. As far

as Jennifer was concerned, Petunia was a three-hundred-pound porcine nightmare that was not going to end anytime soon.

This was not how Jennifer had anticipated spending her summer. But when her older sister, Miranda, called three days ago asking for help with a difficult pregnancy, Jennifer had taken vacation time from her job as a forensic accountant, packed up her seven-year-old son, Zack, and left Dallas.

She'd moved from Blossom the summer after high school, and aside from brief visits home to see her sister and bury her mother, she'd stayed away. There were too many bad memories here. And she wouldn't have come back now, but Miranda and her daughter, Kelly, were family—outside of Zack, the only family Jenn had.

Petunia gave a squeal of displeasure, pulling Jenn out of her reminiscences. She watched as the very pregnant pig struggled to her feet and knocked over her water bowl.

The last thing Jenn wanted to do was climb into the pen with a grouchy pig, but Kelly and Zack had gone to get sodas twenty minutes before, leaving Jennifer to wait for Kelly's 4H adviser.

Jennifer smiled, remembering the scowl on Kelly's face when Zack had signed that he'd go with his cousin and Jennifer had translated for Kelly. No teenager wanted to haul a little boy around with her when she might run into her friends, but Kelly would have to get used to it, at least for a few months. Jennifer would need Kelly's help looking out for Zack, especially after the baby arrived.

It was important that Zack learn to get around despite his deafness. He was usually shy about straying from her side, and when he showed some independence, Jennifer encouraged it. She just wished her niece had been more open to Jenn's offer to teach her sign language so Kelly could communicate with her cousin.

Petunia nosed at her water bowl, her squeals escalating. She sounded as if she was being mistreated in some horrible way.

With no sign of Kelly, Jenn had little choice but to go into the pen and refill the water bowl. She had never raised a pig, but she knew from growing up in Blossom, Texas, that an overheated animal, especially a sow close to giving birth, could spell trouble.

The problem was that Petunia hated to be penned and had become an escape artist. Jenn found the bag of dog biscuits in Kelly's canvas bag, slipped a few into her pocket, then tossed a handful across the pen to lure Petunia away from the door.

While the pig rooted in the hay for the treats, Jennifer let herself inside and closed the gate behind her. Just as she was congratulating herself on keeping the pig penned, she stepped in a soft pile of droppings hidden under the straw. Petunia chose that moment to sniff at Jenn's pocket, smearing her white shorts with a mixture of mushy dog biscuit and pig saliva.

Jennifer heard the low rumble of male laughter

right behind her and froze. Without even turning around she knew who that laugh belonged to. Trace McCabe. The one person she had hoped to avoid during her stay in Blossom.

Recollections of his smile and laugh flashed through her memory like summer lightning. Memories of the hurt and confusion her decisions had caused stung like the sparks coming off a Fourth-of-July sparkler.

Her stomach flipped and her hands began to sweat. Trace McCabe.

The reason she'd stayed away for eight years.

She hadn't seen him since the night they'd gotten married.

She knew she'd been silly to think she could be in Blossom all summer and not see him, but she hadn't wanted to face the memories and feelings she'd avoided for so long.

What had happened between them should stay in the past quietly buried. She had no inclination to dig it up.

She took a deep breath and reached for her composure, plastering on what she hoped was a neutral expression.

Her hesitation cost her as the annoyed pig gave her a shove that sent her stumbling against the side of the enclosure. Petunia moved in quickly and pinned Jenn in the corner.

A big pair of warm hands grasped her upper arms, lifted her and hauled her backward, clear over the top of the pen.

She turned, and knew the moment he recognized her. His easy grin turned into a stunned expression.

She looked up at him, forcing a smile. Dangerous thoughts and emotions shook her. He was bigger, more handsome and so dearly familiar. Time had been very kind to Trace. The trim khaki sheriff's uniform showed off his lean, broad-shouldered body.

Darn! Why couldn't he have gotten fat, or bald?

Her stomach jittered just as it used to when she was seventeen. Perhaps her feelings hadn't been buried as deeply as she'd thought.

Expressions of disbelief and shock chased across his face, followed by a flash of anger. He quickly recovered his composure and gave her a forced smile that didn't look as if it belonged on his tanned face.

The air between them seemed to shimmer.

"Hey there, Trace," she said, amazed her voice sounded so normal.

She could feel her heart racing. She fought the urge to simply turn and walk away from him, get in her car and head for home.

Not an option, she thought. Not this time. She'd run from her responsibilities—from him—once before. She wouldn't run again.

Time for plan B, she thought, resigned. Maybe she could act as if they were just old friends. She forced a smile and said, "How's it going?"

Trace let go of Jenn and stepped back. He felt as if he'd gotten hold of a live wire. He was having trouble getting a deep breath past the ball of anger that flared in his chest.

When he'd walked into the stock barn at the end of his shift and spotted the woman standing in the pigpen, he'd had no idea it was Jenn. She was wearing clothes that belonged at a country club, not in a pigpen. Her sophisticated hairstyle hadn't come from the local beauty shop, and she had sandals on.

Anyone who grew up in Blossom knew you wore boots in a stock barn.

She'd changed a lot in eight years. Her body was more slender and she wore her once-long hair in a tousled, streaked style.

After all this time, thinking about her and wondering, she was standing right in front of him, smiling and greeting him as if they'd seen each other yesterday. As if they'd been casual friends.

Fury streaked through him.

He took off his hat and ran his hand through his hair. "Hey, Jenn. What brings you back to Blossom?"

He struggled to match her casual attitude and give himself a moment to round up his feelings. It was going to take some doing, but if that was how she wanted to play this first meeting, he'd go along. His emotions were in such a turmoil he honestly didn't trust himself to do otherwise. She looked sophisticated and snooty. Dallas had rubbed off on her.

He realized he was slapping his hat against his leg, and he stopped the motion.

Her eyes were just the same. A deep amber color.

The same color as the topaz earrings he'd bought her on his way back to Blossom, before he'd known she'd run off to Dallas and left him behind. He kept those earrings in a box in his dresser. They served as a reminder of his lack of judgment where women were concerned.

She shrugged one tanned shoulder and said, "Miranda needs some help this summer, so I decided to spend my vacation in Blossom."

He'd known she'd stayed in Dallas after college. In a small town like Blossom he didn't need to ask questions about her. Everybody's business was common knowledge, shared regularly at the Bee Hive Cafe, the Dairy Dream and the Alibi Saloon.

He gestured to her shorts with his hat. "I never thought I'd see you in a pigpen."

"Momma is probably turning in her grave. But you know Miranda. If Momma didn't like it, my big sister was all over it," she said, her voice holding a hint of sadness.

Oh, Trace remembered Jenn's mother, he thought with bitterness. Not an easy woman. Jenn's sister had fought her mother every inch of the way, but Jenn had always gone along with whatever her mother wanted. Including breaking it off with him.

Eight years ago he'd blamed her mother for what had happened between them. He'd had plenty of time to grow up and realize Jenn had made decisions, too. The annulment might have been Mrs. Williams's idea, but Jenn hadn't fought against it. She'd never even answered his letters or phone calls or made any effort to contact him.

No matter how he'd felt about or her daughter, he knew his manners.

Mrs. Williams hadn't thought much of Trace, and she'd let him know he wasn't good enough for her daughter, but Trace knew losing a parent was hard. "I was sorry to hear about your mother passing."

Jenn's smile faltered. "Thanks."

They stood awkwardly for a few heartbeats. He wanted answers to so many questions. Answers that would help him let go of the feelings he hadn't realized until now he'd been hauling around for eight years.

The squeal of the pig reminded him they were standing in the middle of a barn. Now was not the time or place to bare his soul to Jenn.

"So, you'll be in town for a while?" He needed to talk to her, but he wasn't going to open their can of worms here in the pig barn.

She nodded. "For the fair. Miranda is off her feet until the baby comes, so I'm going to take on Kelly and Miss Cranky here." She gestured to the pig, who was busy scooting her empty water dish around the pen and complaining.

He wondered if it was hard for her to see her sister pregnant, if it made her think of the child they had lost that summer after she'd graduated from high school. Maybe she'd been able to move on, but the unfinished business between them still gnawed at him.

He reached into the enclosure and grabbed the

dish as the pig went by. He handed it to Jenn. "Well, I've got to get along. You staying with Miranda?"

She nodded, her head bent down, looking at the stainless steel bowl as if it held some fascination for her.

"I'll be in touch."

She glanced up at him with a resigned look on her face. "Okay."

They both knew they needed to have a conversation they should have had eight years ago.

Chapter Two

Trace strode away from Jenn, still trying to get his emotions under control. He wanted to put his fist through a wall.

Hey, Trace, how's it going? What kind of a greeting was that after almost eight years? He jammed his sunglasses back on and stomped out of the swine barn into the blazing sunshine.

They had been as close as two people could be. He had loved her so much he'd ached with it. Was he the only one who remembered that? Had he been harboring the remnants of some adolescent crush all these years? Obviously his emotions had been deeply buried, surfacing to smack him unexpectedly now. Now he had no idea what to do about them.

He stepped into the judging barn and headed for

the fair offices. He needed to find Stan, the 4H adviser. Trace had offered to help out with checking in the projects, but he wasn't going to deal with Kelly's pig—or Jenn—until he had some time to figure out what was going on in his head and how he was going to handle it. Stan would have to check in Kelly's project.

Over at the stock pens, where animals waited for the vet, a child climbing up the slats had Trace changing direction.

The boy, his back to Trace, was on a pen that held a particularly nasty bull from the rodeo herd. He had a broken horn and a bad attitude, along with a habit of charging the fence.

"Hey, kid, get down off there!" Trace broke into a run as the bull turned and spotted the child.

When the boy didn't respond, Trace hollered again. "You, kid, in the red shirt, jump down!"

The boy continued to ignore him. The bull's head was down and Trace could hear him snorting from twenty feet away. Trace closed the distance in record time and snagged the little boy around the waist, jerking him off the pen.

The sound of ripping fabric was quickly drowned out by the bull crashing into the fence, his horns raking the wood with a splintering screech.

Trace backed up, set the boy down and spun him around. "What were you thinking?" he yelled. The boy's terrified freckled face didn't look familiar.

The child looked up at Trace, but said nothing. His whole body shook.

"Who are you here with?" Trace moved the child another few steps away as the bull readied himself for another run at the boards. Whoever was supposed to be supervising this boy was doing a bad job.

The child turned to bolt, then flinched when Trace reached down to keep him in his place. Just as he placed a hand on the boy's shoulder someone called his name.

"Trace, stop!"

He saw Jenn ran toward them, looking as scared as the boy.

"Don't hurt him."

Hurt him?

She arrived panting and out of breath, and scooped the boy into a hug. His little arms went around her shoulders and his legs gripped her waist as he buried his face against her neck.

"What did you think I was going to do? Give him a beating?"

"No, oh, no. Sorry. I was scared."

He nodded, but the notion that she thought he would hurt a child stung.

"Thank you," she said, gulping air as she patted the boy on the back.

"Who is this kid?"

"My son, Zack." She continued to stroke the boy's thin little back.

For the second time that day Trace felt as if he'd been smacked by a two-by-four. Jenn had a child?

She smoothed a hand over Zack's curly brown hair, as if to reassure herself he was all right. "He was supposed to stay with Kelly, but she came back alone."

How come he'd never heard that Jenn had a child? Feeling as twisted up as old hay wire, Trace shoved his hands into his pockets. "I yelled at him to get down, but he ignored me."

Jenn's big hazel eyes filled with tears. "He didn't hear you. Zack is deaf." She lowered the boy back onto his feet, and used sign language to ask him something. Zack pointed to the front of his red shirt, where there was a big hole.

Jenn looked up at Trace. "He was trying to get down, but he got stuck."

There was a piece of the boy's shirt hanging from a splinter on the fence post. "He never should have been there in the first place."

Jenn nodded, and had started to say something when Zack shook her hand to get her attention. He pointed to his shirt and then signed something.

Jenn laughed and nodded, signing back and speaking to him. The child watched her lips. "I know it's your favorite. We can get you another one."

Trace took another look at the boy's red shirt and realized it had the Chicago Bulls' mascot on the front.

The boy made some motions with his hands, and Jenn translated.

"Zack said he's sorry. He wants to thank you."

Trace nodded at the boy, then looked up at Jenn, still trying to absorb the fact that she had a child.

She gave him a wobbly smile and said, "I want to thank you, too. I'll keep him with me in the future." She took Zack's hand and walked away.

Trace watched them leave, and slowly withdrew his hands from his pockets. He wasn't very good at guessing ages, but the boy looked as if he could be about seven.

The same age the child they had supposedly lost would be.

Trace started after them. He needed answers. Now.

His phone beeped. He pulled it out of his pocket, saw the "911" designation and swore under his breath. As much as he needed to confront Jenny, his job called. He flipped open the phone and barked, "What?" He didn't take his eyes off Jenn or Zack until they disappeared from sight.

There was a moment of silence and then his dispatcher, Henrietta, said, "Sheriff?"

Trace ran a hand over his face. "Sorry, Henrie. What's up?"

"Accident on the highway, four miles south of the fairgrounds. Butch thinks one driver might be drunk."

"Any injuries?" Trace glanced at his watch. Geez, it was ten o'clock in the morning.

"Doesn't look too bad, but one of the passengers is trapped in the car. I already dispatched an ambulance, but Butch needs help. And there was another vandalism call, but that can wait until you get in."

Henrie had managed the sheriff's office since before Trace was born. He trusted her judgment completely.

"Tell Butch I'm on my way." Trace shoved his phone into his pocket and headed to his cruiser.

Gripping Zack's hand, Jenn hurried away from Trace and the feelings he awakened in her.

For so long she had tried not to think about him or any of the memories that went with him, but seeing his concern for her son brought those unwanted emotions flooding back. She tried to push them away into the back of her mind where she'd locked them. They didn't seem to fit any longer.

Zack made a growling noise tugged and tugged free of her grasp. "Are you angry with me?" he signed.

She shook her head. "No. Why do you think that?"

He rubbed the hand she'd been holding. "Because you were smashing my hand."

In her agitation she'd had too strong a hold on him. She scooped him up, reveling in the little-boy smell of him. He wiggled out of her grasp as she set him down again. "I'm not angry at you." But she was furious at Kelly. Jenn had given her niece strict instructions to keep an eye on Zack.

Zack signed again. "The man was angry."

"He was frightened for you."

Zack shook his head in disbelief. "Policemen don't get scared."

She nodded, amused by Zack's childlike view of the world, and took him more gently by the hand. She didn't want to talk about Trace. Or why, if Trace was angry at anyone, it was her. Instead, she walked Zack back to the pigpen.

Kelly was sitting on a stool beside Petunia, talking on a cell phone. She didn't look up at them.

Jenn pointed Zack to the empty pen opposite them, where he had been playing earlier with his assortment of action figures. Once he was absorbed, she said. "Kelly, I need to speak to you."

Kelly rolled her eyes and pointed to the telephone.

Jenn barely resisted the urge to rip it out of her hand. "Tell them you'll call them back."

Kelly turned away and said something Jenn couldn't hear, then disconnected the call. When she turned back she had a sullen look on her face. "What?"

Jenn wondered briefly what had happened to the sweet girl who had stayed at her house in Dallas last summer. Kelly had changed from a sunny child to a sullen teenager in the course of a few months.

"I told you how important it was to keep an eye on Zack. He's not like other children."

Kelly shrugged. That insolent lift of her shoulder was becoming a familiar thing. "It's not my fault. I thought he was right behind me."

"Well, he wasn't. He wandered away and was almost gored by a bull."

Kelly glanced over at Zack. "But he wasn't."

"No. Thanks to Trace."

"He should stay with you. I can't talk to him."

"Yes, you can. He's getting good at lip-reading.

"I didn't want him to tag along." Kelly's pretty face got red and blotchy.

"This summer really sucks. I don't see why you even had to come. I can take care of myself." The girl stood up so quickly she knocked her stool over. "It is, like, so disgusting."

Jenn didn't know what she was referring to. "What is?"

Kelly did the eye roll that was becoming annoyingly familiar. "Mom having a baby. She's, like, so old. And just because she has to stay home doesn't mean I can't take care of myself."

Jenn could tell Kelly was trying hard not to cry. Poor kid was having a rough time since her stepfather had walked out on them, but Jenn couldn't let Kelly take it out on her or Zack. "Well, Kel," she said gently, "it would be tough to haul a three-hundred-pound pig to the fairgrounds on the city bus."

Kelly glared at Jenn. "You're as bad as Mom!"

Ah. A truly teenage insult, Jenn thought as she watched her niece turn and run toward the sunlight streaming through the stock-barn doors.

Kelly had been through so much during the past few months. Her stepfather, the only father she remembered, had run off with another woman. According to Miranda, Roger hadn't even said goodbye to Kelly before he moved out, nor had he talked to her since. Add all that to a raging case of hormones, and this was not shaping up to be Kelly's finest summer.

Jenn had nothing but sympathy for her niece's situation. She suspected this was not going to be her best summer, either.

"Jennifer?"

A male voice startled her out of her thoughts. She looked up at a vaguely familiar face.

He held out a hand. "I'm Stan. Stan Donnely. I was in Miranda's class."

She hadn't seen him for years, but she remembered him. He had been a close friend of Miranda's first husband. When Rob had died, Stan had helped with the arrangements. "Of course. Stan. How are you?" She shook his hand.

"I'm fine. How's Miranda?"

Jenn didn't miss the look of genuine concern on Stan's face. "She's on bed rest."

"I'll stop by later and see if she needs me to do anything around the place."

Jenn nodded. "Miranda would appreciate that." Stan had always been a nice guy. He'd never married, and Jenn had suspected he'd had a crush on Miranda since high school.

"Where's Kelly?" He motioned with his clipboard to Petunia. "I'm here to check in her project."

Stalling, giving herself time to think, Jenn said, "Are you the 4H adviser?"

He nodded and smiled. "Yup."

Jenn decided to cover for Kelly. "I sent her to get me a soda. Does she need to be here, or can you do this without her?"

"She needs to be here. I can get started, but I'll bet she'll want to be here for the birth."

Jenn looked at him blankly. Miranda was not due for weeks. "Birth?"

He gestured toward Petunia, who lay on her side panting. "Unless I miss my guess, she's in labor."

In the wake of everything that had happened in the past hour Jenn had forgotten the pig was pregnant. What did you do for a pig in labor?

Stan chuckled and said, "Relax. She knows what to do."

"I hope so." Jenn glanced at Zack, who was still playing across the aisle, then dug her cell phone out of her bag and dialed Kelly's number, praying the girl would pick up.

On the fourth ring Kelly answered, with a rude "What?" Obviously she'd recognized her aunt's number on the incoming call.

Jenn said cheerfully, "Kelly, sweetheart, you'll have to forget my soda. You need to hurry back. Mr. Donnely is here to check Petunia in and he thinks she's in labor."

She heard a yelp and then the line went dead. Jenn smiled up at Stan. "She's on her way."

As they waited for Kelly they chatted about her job in Dallas and how hot the weather was getting. Then the conversation, as it tended to do with old acquaintances, turned to the past.

"You used to go with Trace McCabe, didn't you?"

Jenn tried not to wince at the question. The last

thing she wanted was to discuss Trace. "Yes, for the last two years of high school." People in small towns never forgot anything, Jenn thought.

"Have you seen him since you've been back?"

She nodded and struggled to keep her tone light. "Sure did. He stopped by just a bit ago." She actually managed to make it sound as if it had been no big deal.

She wanted this conversation to be over. It was hard enough to keep her thoughts away from Trace without any reminders.

Stan droned on about the sheriff and the great job he was doing while Jenn kept a pleasant look plastered on her face.

After all, that is what her mother had taught her, she thought with a feeling of rising panic. Self-control. No matter what was going on, keep your face composed and don't give anyone "something to talk about." As if being talked about was the worst thing that could happen to a person.

Jenn's pleasant expression was about to crack when Kelly finally ran toward them, straw and dust flying as her feet pounded the dusty corridor.

Breathless, she said, "Mr. Donnely. I was just getting my aunt a soda." She threw Jenn a grateful look and let herself into the pen.

Jenn led Zack to the end of the pen, and they settled down on a bale of hay to wait for Petunia to get through her ordeal.

Her son, always full of questions, was bound to

be asking some interesting ones today. Jenn sighed and put her arm around Zack. Her quiet summer in Blossom had developed into a whole lot more than she had anticipated.

Chapter Three

Jenn sat on the porch swing in the dark, enjoying the quiet night sounds. It was so comfortable in the house she'd grown up in, and so different to what she'd become accustomed to, living in the city.

Miranda and her second husband, now referred to by the sisters as Roger the Rat, had moved in a few years ago after their mother died. Miranda had, surprisingly, changed very little about the house. In fact, Jenn thought, the entire neighborhood had changed very little since she'd been away.

A light went on in the house across the street. She could see the rooster wallpaper in Mrs. Kincade's kitchen. She smiled at the sight.

Her neighborhood in Dallas was so impersonal. She hardly knew the people who lived on either side of her and had never been in their homes. A week ago she hadn't thought anything about the fact that her neighbors weren't a part of her life. Now, with memories of a different lifestyle pressing in on her, she wasn't so sure her neighborly distance was a good thing.

If she was already questioning her choices, then she'd obviously needed this time to unwind. She took a sip of her lemonade and watched headlights turn into the driveway.

Whatever peace she'd hoped to find tonight was gone. She knew it was Trace even before she saw the light rack on top of the sheriff's car.

He'd always been a bulldog when it came to seeing things through to the end. It was one of the qualities about him she'd always admired, and one that had made the pain eight years ago even worse.

Wouldn't a man as determined as Trace have come after her when she'd left without saying goodbye? Since she'd been the one to leave, it had been childish of her to feel hurt. But back then she'd expected him to come after her—if he'd truly loved her. He must have been relieved when she'd left. He was off the hook. No more playing at husband or father.

But that was eight long years ago. Now all she felt was an odd ambivalence. She didn't want to dredge up the past. She'd buried it, and she intended it to stay that way. No one in Blossom knew of her less-than-two-week marriage to Trace. The secret had died with her mother.

Jenn had told Miranda about losing the baby, but

couldn't bring herself to mention the quick trip over the state line to get married. It had been a childish mistake she wanted to forget.

The night they'd married, Trace had dropped her off at her house, then made the long drive back to San Antonio to his summer job. They'd agreed she'd live with her mother and keep the marriage a secret until he'd earned enough to rent an apartment. Then he'd come home and find a job in Blossom.

But everything had changed when she'd lost the baby a few days later.

Her mother had found out what they'd done. They'd forged a note saying Jenn had her mother's permission to wed, then snuck over the state line and gotten married in New Mexico. Jenn's mother had insisted she get an annulment, and, in the emotional aftermath of the miscarriage, Jenn had agreed.

Now Trace's car pulled up to the front of the house. He killed the lights, but didn't get out. She couldn't see him, but she knew he was staring at her. She could feel his eyes. He knew she was in the shadows of the porch, just as she'd known it was him in the car. They'd always had that kind of connection. It seemed they still did, in spite of everything.

He opened the door and unfolded his tall frame from the driver's seat. He walked slowly up to the porch.

She recognized his rolling gait. He had grown taller and filled out since high school, but she'd know his walk anywhere. To her annoyance, her heart speeded up.

He stopped at the steps without walking up.

"Hey, Trace," she greeted him in a soft voice.

"Jenn."

Just her name, that was all. From the way he said it she could tell he was angry.

He continued to stand there, staring at her. In the old days he would have taken the stairs two at a time, sat down beside her, pulled her into his lap and kissed her breathless.

The thought made her breasts tingle, and a stab of yearning went through her. She had to fight the urge to invite him to sit down beside her.

No one had ever made her feel like Trace had. But she didn't want or need the feelings, and she hadn't, not for a long time.

Finally he cleared his throat. "Is he mine? Is Zack my son?"

Jenn nearly fell off the swing in surprise. "No. Why would you think that?"

He ran his hand over his face. "He's about the right age, isn't he?"

The fact that he was right about Zack's age didn't stop the hurt welling up inside her. Did he really think she could do that to him? Have his child and not tell him?

"I lost our baby, Trace," she said in a shaking voice.

She saw his shoulder lift in a tired shrug. "I hoped—I had to know. He looks like me."

Her anger fizzled, leaving her feeling tender and bruised. Zack *did* look like Trace. Jenn had noticed that about the little boy immediately. She'd had to admit, even at the time of the adoption, it was one of the reasons Zack had quickly become so dear to her.

He let out a soft huff of breath. "Your mother told me about the baby, but she never liked me. I couldn't trust— When I came back to Blossom you'd already gone. She told me she was taking care of the annulment, too, because you were underage."

Only now, as an adult, did Jenn realize how much it must have hurt him, that she'd left without an explanation. "I'm sorry."

She felt sadness wash over her for what they'd lost to their youthful mistakes and her mother's schemes. She wanted Trace to hold her so she could feel the comfort of his strong arms and wide chest.

But she stayed where she was. Those days were long over.

She and Trace were so different now. She was a mother, living in a city she loved. He was a bachelor, and a small-town boy. He'd always lived in Blossom. He hated cities.

Most likely, even if they'd stayed together, their relationship wouldn't have worked. She didn't question why she'd held fast to that belief.

Trace's voice drew her out of her musings.

"I called your mother's house, but she wouldn't talk to me. Then I heard you'd gone off to school. When I found out you'd left for college I went to find you."

"You came to SMU?" She hadn't known he'd tried to contact her after she'd left. It didn't change the present, but knowing he'd come after her untied one of the little knots of sadness she'd held on to for years.

"Yeah. But when I came to my senses and realized *you'd* left *me,* I gave up and came home. I got good and drunk, and then the next day I joined the marines."

"Miranda told me you enlisted."

After a long silence he said, "Nothing went the way we expected, did it?"

His voice held a quiet sadness that tore at Jenn's heart. She resisted the pull. She built a life that fit her needs. She had everything under control. She loved her job, and her son was in a good school. They were a family. They belonged in Dallas, not here in Blossom or with Trace.

"We were so young. I don't think it would have worked," she said softly

Even in the dark she saw the tension in his body. "Why don't you say what you really mean, Jenn?"

She flinched at the anger and resentment in his voice.

"An unplanned baby, an unplanned wedding. What happened between us wasn't *planned* at all. For you, everything worked out for the best."

His words stunned her. "Do you think I *wanted* what happened?"

"No. But I think you wished none of it had ever happened at all."

She wanted to disagree with him, but he'd hit on a secret guilt she'd carried for eight years.

After a long silence he said sadly, "Well, we'll

never know if it would have worked, will we? Good night, Jenn."

He turned and walked back to his car.

For eight years she'd been telling herself things had turned out for the best. But now she wondered, if that was the case, why did she wish deep down, that things had turned out differently?

The next morning, as Zack watched cartoons in the living room, Jenn listened as her sister pointed out the things she wanted removed from the room that was going to be the baby's nursery.

This had been Roger's den, and Miranda was trying to remove every trace of her husband. Jenn didn't blame her. He'd run off with an eighteen-year-old hairdresser, and neither Jenn nor Miranda were in a particularly forgiving state of mind.

"What do you want me to do with the stuff he left behind?" Jenn asked as she surveyed the fishing equipment, piles of magazines and baseball shoes, gloves and bats.

"Put it at the curb. Tomorrow is garbage day."

"I don't know, Miranda. Do you really want to throw it away?"

Miranda rubbed her belly and laughed, but the sound held little humor. "That's exactly what I want."

"Okay." Jenn bit the inside of her cheek to keep from telling Miranda that the contents of their trash pile would be talked about all over Blossom. Jenn hated it when she heard her mother's words coming out of her own mouth. "You go put your feet up. I'll dig in here," she said instead. She was worried for her sister. Miranda tired easily, and last night Jenn had heard her crying. From the dark circles under Miranda's eyes, Jenn was sure her sister was sleeping badly, when she slept at all.

Now Miranda didn't even argue. She turned and left the room.

Jenn spent the next hour piling things by the door. From the back of the closet she dragged out an old dress box from a Dallas store that had gone out of business years ago. It was sealed with tape, coated with dust and marked with their mother's name.

Curious, she wiped the box with a rag, then carried it upstairs to Miranda's bedroom. Her sister looked up from the book she was reading.

"There's a box with Mom's name on it. I thought we went through everything after she died." Jenn put the box on the bed.

Miranda pushed herself up against the headboard. "Roger found that in the rafters in the garage about a year ago and brought it into the house. I kept meaning to go through it, but never got around to it."

"Are you up to it now?"

"Sure."

Jenn went back downstairs to the office and began to scrub the walls of the closet.

A few minutes later Miranda appeared at the office door holding a large manila envelope. "Jenn, you need to see this."

Jenn dropped her sponge into the bucket and wiped her wet hands on her jeans. She took the envelope from her sister and slid out the papers. The date on the cover sheet was eight years old. It was a checklist of information that would be needed to complete an annulment. And the original, completed forms filled out with Trace's and her names. Jenn's knees felt weak and she sat down on the desk chair. As she stared at the form, the realization of what she held in her hand sank in.

The final papers for her annulment had never been filed.

Miranda lifted the papers from Jenn's numb fingers, then picked up the envelope and studied the postmark. "This must have come the week Mom was diagnosed. I remember, because we went to the doctor on Kelly's birthday."

Jenn nodded. She'd never forget that phone call. "You called me at school to tell me about Mom. I was studying for midterm exams."

She covered her mouth with both hands and mumbled through her fingers. "Oh, my gosh. Do you know what this means?"

Miranda skimmed the papers again and gave Jenn an evil little smile. "I suspect you and Trace McCabe are still legally married. So what are you going to do?"

Jenn reached for the phone. "First of all, I'm going to make sure I'm *not* legally married," she said in a voice full of bravado.

Then, she thought with a sinking feeling, if her instincts were right, she was going to have to tell her husband the truth.

Chapter Four

Jenn sat in her car outside Trace's house. It was old, but the wood siding and trim sported a fresh coat of paint, and the walk was bordered with neatly tended flower beds. The sheriff's car was parked in the driveway.

Catching Trace at home was better than meeting him at his office. After all, she wanted privacy when she dropped her bomb, didn't she?

She got out of her car and nervously smoothed the skirt of her yellow sundress. Taking a deep breath, she rang the doorbell and listened to it chime inside the house. When there was no response, she rang again. All she got was an unnerving silence. Butterflies churned in her stomach.

Had he seen her arrive and decided not to answer

the door? The thought bothered her. Even though she'd begun her visit to Blossom wanting to avoid him, she irrationally didn't want him treating her the same way. Especially now that they'd crossed paths and exchanged words.

She had raised her hand to knock, to give it one last try, when she heard the unmistakable cough and sputter of a gas lawn mower starting up.

She listened for a moment. The noise was coming from the back of the house. She blew out a little sigh of relief. He wasn't ignoring her. He must be mowing his yard.

She stepped down off the front porch and walked across the lawn to the driveway, headed toward the uneven growl of the mower. As she cleared the side of the house and got a full view of the backyard, she stopped dead.

Trace had his back to her, pushing an ancient mower through tall grass. He wore nothing but a pair of shorts that sat low on his hips, and sneakers without socks. The muscles of his arms and shoulders stood out as he wrestled the mower. Glistening, sweaty muscles that had not been on his lean frame eight years ago.

She swallowed, her mouth suddenly dry.

The body she remembered had belonged to a lanky twenty-year-old boy on the brink of manhood. The body that held her attention now was fully matured, filled out and beautifully sculpted.

As he turned the mower to make another pass, he

didn't look up and she stayed in the shadows, watching.

He had grown quite a lot of hair on his chest. It was curly like the hair on his head. She swallowed again and felt the tips of her fingers tingle as she remembered how she'd loved to touch him.

Dangerous, forbidden feelings surfaced like hot water bubbling out of a thermal spring. She couldn't seem to take her eyes off him or forget no other man had ever made her feel the way Trace had.

She'd told herself over the years that she'd exaggerated her memories of him. It was only normal. After all, Trace had been her first love and she'd been an inexperienced teenager with overactive hormones. Of course he'd seemed exciting, passionate, wonderful.

So why did she suddenly think he might still all of those things, and possibly more?

She looked down, fiddling with the tie at the waist of her dress as she tried to compose herself.

She didn't need those kinds of thrills. She didn't want them. A relationship with that much passion was too complicated, too messy and took up far too much time.

She had her life right where she wanted it. And it didn't—couldn't—include Trace.

The sound of the idling mower caught her attention. Trace had spotted her.

He stood in the middle of his yard like a bronzed statue. His large hands clutched the handle of the unmoving mower, and he was staring at her.

She couldn't read the expression on his face. He seemed distant. It shouldn't bother her, but it did.

Jenn pasted on a smile and stepped into the sunshine, hoping he would think she had just arrived. "Hey, Trace."

He leaned over the mower and shut it off. The sun glistened in his hair, and bits of grass clung to his sweaty skin. He straightened, and the silence that stretched between them seemed very loud.

She took a hesitant step forward, then said in a rush, "I need to talk to you, but you're busy. I can come back." Chicken, she scolded herself.

He shook his head, then wiped his arm across his forehead. "Now is fine. I could use a break."

He left the mower in the middle of the yard and picked up a hose, dousing himself with water and then shaking like a dog.

He'd always been so at home with himself, a quality Jenn, who usually felt self-conscious, admired.

As Trace picked up a T-shirt hanging from the back porch railing and dried himself off, she tried her best not to stare. What was she doing, alone with a half-naked man? She could almost hear her mother's often-voiced refrain: what will the neighbors think?

Jenn glanced around and realized Trace had no neighbors within sight. She could grab him right here, outside, and there would be no one to see.

Now she had managed to shock herself.

"Jenn? Something wrong?" Trace pulled the rumpled shirt over his head.

"No! Everything's fine." She shook her head. At least he had removed the visual temptation.

"Well, not exactly fine," she said. Where did she begin?

Politely, still keeping his distance, he motioned toward the back door. "Come on in. Let's get out of the sun. I've got cold sodas in the fridge." He climbed the back steps and toed off his grass-caked shoes.

He held the door for her and she stepped past him into a tiny utility room. He smelled like sunshine and grass and sweaty man. A tempting combination.

Trace ushered her into a tidy kitchen with clean white counters and white appliances. A row of windows looked out on the backyard and a round wooden table sat on the terra-cotta tile floor. The only thing that looked out of place was the holstered gun sitting in the middle of the table.

"Soda?" He was still watching her with that unreadable expression on his face.

She wanted to tell him she didn't plan to be here that long, but manners had her saying, "Thank you. Diet if you have it."

He looked her up and down, and her temperature rose several degrees. He shook his head as he reached in and pulled out two red cans. "No diet."

Did he mean he didn't have diet, or she didn't need it?

He popped the lid on one of the cans and handed it to her, then propped his lean hips against the counter next to the stove and opened his own can.

She was staring down at his bare feet, wondering where to start, when his voice brought her back.

"Do you want to sit down?"

Abruptly she met his gaze. "No. This will just take a minute." Like ripping off a bandage, it would be better to get it done quickly.

Jenn took a deep breath and said, "Miranda and I were cleaning out a room for the baby and I found a box of papers in a closet." She stopped and took a sip of soda, needing to wet her suddenly dry throat.

He nodded, a puzzled look on his face.

She lowered the can of soda and said, "There was an envelope from the state of New Mexico."

At that, his expression and body language changed. He stood up a little straighter and his brow furrowed. He didn't speak, but made a little motion with his hand, encouraging her to continue.

She took a deep breath and let the words rush out. "My mother never completed the forms for our annulment."

He stared at her for so long she had to fight not to squirm. She babbled instead. "I called the number on the form. They checked and…" She let the sentence trail off, not wanting to say the words out loud.

His voice was very quiet. "And what, Jenn?"

She cleared her throat. "We're still married."

Neither one of them moved.

Finally Trace shook his head and set his soda on the counter beside him. He crossed his arms over his chest, his expression still unreadable. "So now what do we do?"

She pasted on a plastic smile. "It's not really a problem. We can file the papers ourselves. There are grounds."

"Desertion?" Trace gave a hard bark of laughter.

"That would work." Yes, it fit. For both of them.

There was a hint of anger in him she'd never seen before. She took a step back, feeling uncertain of this Trace, this man she couldn't read.

Immediately he relaxed against the counter. "Do you want me to take care of it?" he asked in that neutral voice she was beginning to hate.

"No. I'll do it." She headed for the door, needing to get away from him and the feelings that crowded her head. "Thanks for the soda," she said over her shoulder. How inane to be polite after what had just transpired.

"You're welcome," Trace replied just as politely to her back.

She went through the utility room and out the back door, squinting into the bright sunlight. She made her way back to her car, fighting against the urge to cry.

They'd never really been married. He'd stepped up because she was pregnant. They'd never even spent even one night together as Mr. and Mrs. Trace McCabe. So why did she feel as if she'd just lost something?

Key in hand, she slid onto the hot upholstery of

the driver's seat and had to blink away her silly tears to find the ignition.

It was done, and over. Grow up and stop being so maudlin, she told herself. What had happened was eight years in the past.

She had her life in Dallas, the job she'd always wanted and her son. She was happy.

She pulled away from the curb. Telling Trace the truth had gone better than she'd hoped. Very civilized. He'd been…like a stranger.

Instead of feeling elated, she felt as if she'd just lost her lover all over again.

Trace got to the living-room window in time to see Jenn walk down his driveway. How could he be so physically attracted to her when she made him so furious?

He watched her slim hips sway in a purely feminine walk as she made her way to her car. He'd always loved to watch her move.

She walked like a person who had places to go. And she had. She'd gone to Dallas and she'd never come home.

As he watched her pull away from the curb he thought about what she'd just told him. Even though he'd believed the annulment had been finalized years ago, her casual offer to end their marriage had been damn hard to hear.

He turned away and headed toward the bathroom and a shower. As much as he would love to go back out to the yard and work the anger out of his system, duty called. But as he lathered up, his thoughts drifted into dangerous territory.

What if Jenn hadn't lost the baby?

Their child would be the same age as Zack.

Would they have had a successful marriage? More children?

Or was she right? Had they been too young to have it last?

When they had first started dating, Jenn had had big plans for college and a career. He'd been a part of those dreams.

The unplanned pregnancy had upset her, made her feel out of control. He'd never seen her so distressed. And when she lost the baby, she'd gone back to her plans, minus him.

He stuck his head under the spray and called himself a fool for wanting things that could never be.

He had other things he needed to think about, things he could actually do something about. Like the frustrating investigation into the land swindle that had cost several residents of the county thousands of dollars. And the Committee for Moral Behavior was driving him crazy with their demands to make changes "for the good" of Blossom. He knew they meant well, but they didn't seem to understand there was only so much he could do without treading on other people's civil rights.

He dressed, grabbed his weapon and wallet and was stopped twice on his way to his meeting with the mayor.

The town's gardener had found two garden trolls sitting on the bench in front of the courthouse. He wanted Trace to know they were in his shed.

Then Trace ran into the clerk of the court, who needed to show him pictures of her latest grandchild.

The Committee for Moral Behavior was assembled and in full rant by the time he got to the meeting. He didn't miss the matching expressions of displeasure on the faces of Bitsy Dupres, Reverend Tolliver and Minnie Dressler when he walked in.

Bitsy Dupres didn't miss a beat in her tirade as she gave him a look that let him know he was late.

Jason Strong, current mayor and Trace's longtime friend, nodded at him, a bland expression on his face.

Trace took a chair and listened to the same conversation they'd been having for months.

"Since the sheriff is finally here," Bitsy said, "I think we need to address the recent bout of vandalism. The carnival workers are probably responsible."

Trace shook his head. "The thefts of yard ornaments—and I want to point out that all the statuary has been recovered—began long before the carnival people got to Blossom. As I've told you before, I think it's kids. As for the vandalism on the fairgrounds, I'm still investigating."

Bitsy sniffed as if he had offended her and turned her ire on Jason, charging off on another subject, which involved the garbage cans at the park.

Trace listened with half an ear as his mind drifted back to Jenn, and how she had looked in her little yellow sundress standing in his backyard, the sun shining on her hair.

His cell phone vibrated, jarring him out of his thoughts. Thoughts he'd promised himself he wasn't going to have.

The code for the message from Henrie was just what he needed to get himself out of the meeting. He plastered a serious expression on his face. "Sorry, folks, police business. I need to go." He'd much rather be returning garden trolls than listening to the CMB.

Jason nodded at him, then glanced at the others. When he was sure no one was looking, he held up his index finger. It was a sign they'd had for years. Trace hid a grin and nodded at his friend. He owed Jason a beer for leaving the meeting early.

Trace turned and left. He had enough headaches this summer with the swindle, the vandalism, the fair. And Jenn.

The Committee for Moral Behavior was way down on his list. Maybe he would buy Jason two beers, he thought as he headed for his office.

Chapter Five

"Come on, Kelly. It'll be fun!"

A few days after her encounter with Trace, Jenn dragged her reluctant niece to the fortune-teller's big red tent that fluttered with colorful scarves.

They had dropped Zack off at day camp and checked on Petunia and her brood. Jenn would do anything to keep her mind off Trace, even pay for some harmless fun at the fair with a Gypsy fortune-teller.

"Aunt Jenn, you don't believe in that stuff, do you?" Kelly allowed Jenn to drag her along, and Jenn sensed the girl was interested, but reluctant to admit it.

Jenn didn't particularly believe anyone could foresee the future, but she really wanted to get on a better footing with Kelly. Hopefully this outing would inject some fun into their relationship.

Jenn grinned at Kelly. "What can it hurt?"

The front flaps of the tent were rolled up and tied back, and sheer gold panels, cinched in the middle, partially covered the opening. Jenn could see a small table inside holding an honest-to-goodness crystal ball. The psychic, an attractive young woman, motioned them into the tent and told them where to sit.

Jenn wasn't sure what she had expected, but it wasn't this vibrant, beautiful woman with sparkling eyes and an abundance of curly brown hair. She introduced herself as Cherry and brought out the tarot cards.

Jenn turned to Kelly. "You want to go first?"

Kelly shook her head. "This was your idea. You go."

Jenn shrugged and smiled at the psychic. "I guess I'm up."

The woman studied her for a long moment, then said, "Shuffle the cards until you feel that you're ready, then cut the deck into three piles."

Jenn followed the instructions, awkwardly shuffling the big cards. She arranged three neat piles on the table between them.

Cherry pointed at the cards. "Now choose one."

"Any one?" Jenn asked. The whole process seemed a bit mysterious.

Cherry nodded. "The one that feels the best to you."

Jenn wasn't sure exactly what she meant, so she pointed to the stack in the middle.

"Hand them to me."

As the fortune-teller reached for the cards, her hand brushed against Jenn's. The brief touch was warm, and Jenn had the oddest sensation that a current ran between them. She pulled back slightly, feeling silly for her overactive imagination.

The fortune-teller smiled. "I don't bite. And I don't give bad news."

Jenn willed herself to relax. "Okay." She heard Kelly give a quiet snort and she suppressed a smile, not daring to look at her niece for fear of bursting into nervous laughter.

The fortune-teller was silent as she laid out the cards and studied them. Jenn fought the urge to squirm in her chair.

Finally Cherry tapped one of the elaborate drawings. "You came home to heal a hurt. Be open to the silent messages. Some words are hard to speak."

Jenn flinched. Was the woman lucky, or did she really have the skill to see into someone's life?

The fortune-teller closed her eyes. "What you thought was lost is still where you left it. Look closely. You'll be home soon." She gently gathered up the cards and turned to Kelly.

She gave Kelly the same instructions about shuffling and dividing the cards, then said, "Don't be frightened, little one."

Kelly visibly stiffened up.

Oh, no, Jenn thought. Kelly was at an age where she would not admit that anything scared her. Jenn held her breath, sure Kelly would get up and leave. Much to her surprise, Kelly seemed intent on what the woman was saying.

"Someone new will come into your life and you will fall deeply in love this summer." Her brow furrowed and she paused, as if deep in thought. "Twice," the fortune-teller said. Her concentration and puzzlement looked real.

Suddenly her brow smoothed out and she laughed. "Two young men. One love, deep and true and steady, will last all your life. The other will become a pleasant memory."

Oh, great, Jenn thought as she watched Kelly's rapt attention on the fortune-teller. What had she gotten her niece into? Kelly already had enough to keep her off balance emotionally. Now she was going to be looking for Mr. The-Rest-of-Her-Life and Mr. Right-Now.

The fortune-teller took Kelly's hand between both of her own. "Things will get better, little one. Trust yourself, and trust those who love you."

She stood up, signaling the end of the session.

Jenn forced a smile and dropped money on the table. "Thanks. That was fun."

The fortune-teller looked at her with a sad expression, then she smiled again. "Take good care of the little one."

Jenn watched Kelly fish around on the floor for her purse, then leave the booth.

In a low voice the fortune-teller said, "Your sister will be fine, and so will her son." Then she turned and walked through a curtain at the back, disappearing from view.

Jenn stared after her, openmouthed.

"Aunt Jenn?" Kelly's voice brought her around.

She snapped her mouth closed, pasted on a smile and turned to join Kelly outside. "Well, that was fun, wasn't it?"

Kelly shot her an unreadable look as they walked back to the barn. "Do you believe it?"

The woman had hit way too close to the mark for Jenn, but she wasn't about to admit it. "I think it's all an act. I mean, she talked about me going home. Well, sure, I'm going back to Dallas after your mom has the baby. But that was a pretty broad statement."

She wasn't even going to mention the parting comments the woman had made about Miranda and her son. Even Miranda didn't know the sex of the baby. She'd had a sonogram, but had decided to wait and be surprised.

"What about the part where she'd said you'd lost something and you'd find it?"

Jenn did some quick thinking. "I lost my high school ring before I went to college. Maybe it will turn up."

Kelly was quiet as they walked along, their shoes kicking up the dust. "What about what she said about me?"

Jenn gave Kelly's arm a squeeze. "Falling in love? Sure, why not? That was a no-brainer. Any girl as pretty as you will have boys after her."

She didn't miss Kelly's jolt of surprise. "You think?"

"I know!"

"What about the part about you healing a hurt?"

Jenn looked down at her sandals and forced a laugh. "That was a shot in the dark that missed!"

Just then, when they were about fifty yards from the entrance to the barn, she spotted Trace in the distance. He was standing talking to Kelly's 4H adviser, Stan.

Talk about timing.

He was in uniform, his face was shadowed by his hat and mirrored sunglasses hid his eyes.

Kelly spotted him just after Jenn did. "Mom said you dated him in high school. The sheriff."

Dated. Such a benign term, Jenn thought, remembering how her hormones had soared every time she'd caught sight of him. Unfortunately, that hadn't changed much, it seemed. Her nerve endings were already quivering.

"Yup. For two years."

"Wow. He's old, but he's still hot."

Old? Jenn stopped in her tracks and glared at her niece. Old? She stifled a sigh. To Kelly they probably *did* seem old. But she had to agree with her niece's assessment. She'd almost melted into a puddle when she'd seen him in nothing but a pair of shorts yesterday, all sweaty and delicious. Yup. Trace was still hot.

"What happened?" Kelly asked as Jenn caught up with her.

"When?" Jenn asked. She'd lost the thread of the conversation as she'd watched Trace.

"I mean, like, what happened to break you up?"

Jenn pasted on her best "all in the past" expression and gave a casual wave of her hand. "Oh, I went off to college. Trace joined the marines. We lost touch."

"So now you're, like, strangers. Did you think it was going to be forever?"

Oh, yes, Jenn had thought it would be forever. When she was young and naive. She forced a smile for Kelly and spit out the adult party line. "Oh, no. We were way too young. It wouldn't have lasted."

Now they *were* just strangers.

Married strangers.

But would it have worked? If they'd given it a chance? If she'd stood up to her mother? There were so many "what ifs."

Was this what the fortune-teller meant? Could Jenn heal the old hurts? Did she even want to? It was so much easier to put them away and not think about them.

"Aunt Jenn?" Kelly slowed down.

"Hmmm?"

"How do you know when it's forever?"

Poor kid. She'd been so hurt by her stepdad's abandonment she was bound to question the permanency of any relationship. "I have no idea, Kel. I'll let you know when I find out."

When they got to the barn, Stan walked Kelly inside to get more information about Petunia, and Trace put his hand on Jenn's arm. She felt as if she'd been neatly cut out of the herd by an expert cowboy.

Trace watched Stan and Kelly until they had moved out of hearing range. "Where's your son?"

Jenn picked up immediately on the serious tone of his voice. "At day camp, at the Y. What's wrong?"

"I need you to come with me. Miranda just called and she's having some problems."

"What kind of problems?"

He shook his head. "She didn't get specific. She said she couldn't get you on your cell."

"I forgot to put it in my bag this morning." It was still in the charger on the table by her bed.

"She said she didn't want to call Kelly's cell and upset her, so she called me. Can you make an excuse to Kelly?"

"Sure. My car's here." So much for the psychic, she thought in a panic, saying Miranda and her son would be fine.

Trace's voice cut into her thoughts. "I'll take you. You might need me."

"Okay." It would be a lot quicker to leave from here than to go all the way out to the parking lot where she'd left her car.

Jenn hurried into the barn and gave Kelly the first excuse that popped into her head. "Trace and I are going to lunch. I'll come back to get you later."

Kelly gave her a sly smile. "The hottie is taking you out. Go for it, Aunt Jenn!"

Jenn rolled her eyes and shook her head. "Do you have enough money for lunch?"

She grinned. "Yup. Have a good time."

Jenn hurried out to Trace's car.

He didn't say a word as he drove her to Miranda's house. Jenn thought again of the things the fortune-teller had said, things she would like to forget. Be open to the silent messages. Well, they had the silence, she thought as Trace pulled up in the driveway. If only she could figure out the message and how to heal the hurt she knew he was feeling. Was it even possible? The fortune-teller had been wrong about Miranda, and she was probably wrong about Trace, too.

She jumped out of the car as soon as it stopped rolling, Trace following behind her. Miranda was on the couch in the living room, her face as white as the doilies that still protected the old overstuffed furniture. Jenn dropped to her knees and grabbed her sister's hand, which was ice-cold.

"Miranda, honey, what happened?"

"I started having contractions." Her voice was shaky. "I called the doctor and he said to lie down until I could get a ride. Where's Kelly?"

"I made an excuse and left her at the fair. She's fine."

Miranda looked relieved. "Thanks."

"Let's get you to the doctor, and then I'll go get her.

Miranda started to cry, spooking Jenn even more. Miranda never cried.

"He said to come right to the hospital."

Trace pulled Jenn to her feet. "You get the door and I'll take Miranda."

He scooped Miranda off the couch and she gave a little yelp. "Trace McCabe, you put me down. I'm so big I'll give you a hernia."

Trace just laughed and carried Miranda through the doorway. "You questioning my physical condition, Miranda?"

Just like that he had her laughing, and some color came back into her cheeks. Jenn let go of the screen door and ran ahead to open the rear door of the cruiser. Gently he lowered Miranda to the seat and made sure her legs were tucked in before he closed the door. She looked better already.

God bless Trace. He'd always had the ability to make things seem okay. As Jenn slid into the front seat she realized with a jolt how much she had missed having someone to depend on.

Not just someone. Him.

She pushed the thought away. She didn't need him. Her life was just the way she wanted it, the way she'd planned it. She had everything under control. She'd discovered the hard way how painful life could be if you depended on someone else to make things right.

As Trace put the car in gear, she pushed the thoughts of him out of her mind. Right now she needed to think about Miranda.

She refused to make time for anything else.

Chapter Six

Jenn had been tossing and turning for hours. Awake she worried about Miranda, and asleep she dreamed about Trace. Annoyed at herself for letting her worries and dreams get in the way of a good night's sleep, she rolled out of bed and headed to the kitchen for a glass of milk.

At least Jenn didn't have to worry about Zack tonight. He'd met his new best friend at day camp and he was spending the night at the boy's house.

But as she paused in the doorway of her niece's dark bedroom, the bottom dropped out of her stomach. The bed was empty.

The blankets were undisturbed. The windows were closed. Kelly's purse wasn't on the edge of her dresser, where it usually was. Only yesterday Jenn had teased Kelly about always keeping it with her, even at the pig barn.

Jenn went down the hall to Miranda's room. Maybe Kelly was upset about her mother being in the hospital and she'd decided to sleep in her mother's bed.

Miranda's room was empty, too.

Don't panic, she told herself. Just stay calm.

Maybe Kelly was downstairs.

As she searched the house, hoping desperately to find Kelly curled up on a couch or in a chair, she thought back to this evening.

The doctors had stopped Miranda's contractions, but they were going to keep her in the hospital on bed rest. Trace had arranged for Stan to bring Kelly to the hospital, then Trace had brought her and Jenn home. He'd even had someone pick up Jenn's car from the fairgrounds and deliver it to Miranda's house.

Trace had taken care of everything. He'd calmed Miranda with his gentle sense of humor, soothed Kelly and made sure Zack was taken care of.

He'd treated Jenn politely, like a stranger. She didn't want it to hurt, but it did. And now, on top of it all, it seemed Kelly had snuck out of the house.

Jenn searched Kelly's room for an address book, or anything with telephone numbers on it. Kelly's desk and her dresser yielded nothing that might give Jenn a place to start looking.

Oh, Lord, what was she going to tell Miranda? That she had misplaced her daughter? Miranda had strict orders from her doctor to stay in bed and to avoid all stress. What a thing to tell the mother of a teenage daughter!

It was 2:00 a.m. and Jenn had no idea where to find her niece. She couldn't call Miranda and she couldn't call Kelly's stepfather. Roger was in Mexico.

She hadn't forgotten Trace's competence this afternoon. Should she call him? He'd treated her so distantly…. Get a grip, she told herself. This wasn't about her, it was about Kelly.

Jenn remembered being a teenager. She knew what kinds of trouble kids could get into in the middle of the night. On more than one occasion she and Trace had gone to parties that had gotten out of hand.

She dug the Blossom telephone directory out of the pantry and looked up Trace's home number. Putting a shaking finger on his number, she closed her eyes and searched her mind for an alternative. As much as she didn't want to lean on him, she had to admit she couldn't take care of this by herself. She had no idea where the kids went to party these days. It was not the kind of information Kelly would share with her aunt. Trace, as sheriff, was likely to have some ideas.

Jenn found her resolve and reached for the phone. If he wasn't home she'd try the dispatcher, but as desperate as she was to find Kelly, she really didn't want the girl's escapade to be the topic of discussion tomorrow at the Bee Hive or the Cut and Curl.

Jenn punched in the number, and Trace answered on the third ring, his voice husky with sleep.

"McCabe."

The sound of that rough low voice went through her like a bolt of lightning.

She licked her lips. "Ah, Trace. It's Jenn. I'm sorry to wake you."

"Is Miranda okay?" Suddenly he sounded wide awake.

She gulped back an urge to cry. "I'm not calling about Miranda. Kelly is gone."

"What do you mean, gone?"

She heard the rustle of sheets and tried not to think about him in bed. "She's not in her bed."

"How long has she been gone?"

Jenn wiped at a tear that had escaped despite her vow not to cry. "I don't know. She said she had a headache when we got home from the hospital around ten-thirty. I went to bed right after she did."

"Could she have gone back to the hospital?"

Jenn hadn't considered that possibility. "Not without a ride. It's got to be six or seven miles."

"She has friends with cars."

Trace was being so logical it made her feel calmer. "I suppose it's possible, but why wouldn't she tell me she was going?"

"Let me make a call and I'll call you right back," he said in a soothing tone.

"Okay. Thanks." The only answer was the click of his disconnect.

Jenn, determined not to fall to pieces as her mind conjured up all kinds of bad endings, flipped on all the lights in the kitchen and emptied the dishwasher to keep busy. When all the dishes were put away she cleaned out the refrigerator, unwilling to move more than a few feet from the phone on the wall.

When the phone rang she grabbed the receiver and said, "Hello," hoping to hear Kelly's voice.

It was Trace. "She's not at the hospital. I called the nurses' station on Miranda's floor."

Jenn bit the inside of her cheek, trying not to cry, and feeling silly for not thinking of calling the hospital herself.

"I checked with dispatch and there have been two disturbance calls for kids having a loud party."

Finally. Something she could do. "Where? I'll go and see if she's there." Jenn searched the counter for her car keys.

Trace cleared his throat. "I can't let you do that."

"Why not?" Her hand closed over her key chain.

"Because once a call is made it becomes a law enforcement situation. I'm going to take this one. I'll check and see if Kelly's there." He sounded distant and official.

"I want to go with you. Trace, I'm so worried." She blurted out the last part, and wanted to bite her tongue for sounding hysterical.

He made an impatient sound. "Jenn, you're going to have to trust me. I know you want to be in control of this, but you can't."

"But—"

He cut her off. "You stay there. I'll find her." His

voice softened a bit, sounding more like the old Trace. "Try not to worry."

"And if she is at the party? Will you call me so I can come and pick her up?"

"If she's there I'll bring her home," he said reassuringly.

"And if she's not?" Jenn asked with a quaver in her voice she couldn't control.

"Jenn, don't borrow trouble." He hung up.

"Okay." She whispered into the dead line, wishing she could do as he said. Trace hadn't raised children. He didn't know what it was like to worry about them.

Jenn finished cleaning the refrigerator, then went and gathered a load of laundry. She stuffed it into the machine and tried to think positively. She had just finished mopping the kitchen floor when a car pulled up out front. Headlights swept across the dark front room, lingered for a moment, then were shut off.

Jenn tossed the mop into the bucket and raced through the living room to the front door. Trace's cruiser was out front, and he was pulling a giggling Kelly out of the backseat.

Jenn's worry turned to anger. Kelly had been drinking.

The girl spotted Jenn on the porch. "Hey, Aunt Jenn!" She yelled and waved, almost knocking herself over.

"Shh!" Jenn hissed at Kelly "What will the neighbors think?" She slapped her forehead as she heard her mother's words coming out of her mouth.

Kelly stumbled up the driveway, humming as she tripped over her own feet. Jenn reached out to help her up the porch steps and Kelly threw her arms around her. If Trace hadn't grabbed both of them Kelly would have knocked her to the ground.

"I love you, Aunt Jenn," Kelly shouted into her ear. She smelled like stale beer and old cigarette smoke.

Jenn wanted to shake some sense into her, then realized there was no point in a lecture. In the morning Kelly probably wouldn't even remember coming home.

"I love you, too," she said between clenched teeth as she untangled herself from the girl's arms and got her footing. Trace took one side of the teenager and Jenn took the other.

Kelly pointed at Trace and said in a loud whisper, "Did you see who gave me a ride home?"

Jenn nodded and glanced at Trace, who was trying his best not to smile.

Jenn shot him a look that said. *You better not laugh if you know what's good for you,* then turned her attention back to her niece. "Yes, I saw." She took Kelly by the arm and led her toward the stairs.

Kelly stopped abruptly and swayed. She looked over her shoulder at Trace, then back at Jenn. "It's your hottie, Aunt Jenn," she said in a loud whisper. "I got to ride home with your hottie."

Jenn kept her back to Trace as she felt the scorch

of a blush creep up her neck. She steered Kelly inside and to the bathroom, where she stripped the smelly clothes off the girl.

As she was pulling a nightshirt over Kelly's head, the teenager made an odd noise. Jenn jerked the knit shirt into place. Kelly was no longer laughing, and she'd turned an alarming shade of green.

Her niece was now going to pay the price for her misdeeds.

"Okay," she said as she gently pushed the unresisting Kelly down in front of the toilet. "Stay right here until you're finished."

Kelly's only response was to inch closer to the toilet.

Jenn pushed the rug out of range and left her niece on the tile floor.

She hesitated at the door, trying to decide which was worse—staying with Kelly knowing what was about to happen, or facing Trace after Kelly's comments about him being a hottie.

Her hottie.

She leaned her head against the wall, suddenly exhausted. All her fear and anger had become bone-deep fatigue. Had she ever felt this tried and wrung out?

She pulled herself away from the wall and went downstairs. She needed to thank Trace for bringing Kelly home and ask where he had found her. Thinking about an appropriate punishment for Kelly could wait until tomorrow.

The smell of coffee drifted to her as she entered

the kitchen. Trace had his back to her, staring out the window at the dark backyard.

When he heard her come in, he turned and leaned against the counter. He gestured to the coffeemaker. "Hope you don't mind. I'm up for the day." He gave her a long look. "Are you okay?"

Jenn shrugged off his second question. She was too shaky to talk about how she was feeling. "Of course I don't mind," she said, pointing to the coffeepot. "The least I can do is fix you breakfast."

"I'll pass on food, thanks." He reached for the door handle of the cupboard holding the coffee mugs.

It didn't surprise her that he knew where the mugs were. When they'd been dating Trace had been as at home in this kitchen as he'd been in his own mother's.

Jenn watched him pour his coffee. The scene had an oddly comfortable feel to it. Would they have had times like this if they'd made a go of their marriage? Quiet moments of domesticity? She pushed the thought away and said, "I'm sorry about getting you out of bed. I didn't know what else to do."

He waved his hand in a dismissive gesture and gave her a smile. "The dispatcher would have called me in a minute or two anyway to break up the party. How's Kelly?"

Jenn grimaced. "Paying the price. I left her in front of the toilet."

Trace nodded and grinned. "Been there a few times myself."

"You have?" Jenn asked, surprised. As a teenager he'd never had more than a beer or two.

He shrugged. "Rite of passage."

Jenn made a face. "Not me. It never seemed appealing."

Trace gave her a long look. "No, it wouldn't. You never liked to lose control."

His comment annoyed her. She fisted her hands on her hips. "What do you mean by that?"

He put down his steaming mug. "Come on, Jenn. You know what I mean. You get very uncomfortable when things don't go the way you plan them."

His comment stung. He made it sound as if she was a control freak. "I can be flexible!"

He nodded, but she got the feeling it wasn't in agreement with her statement.

Feeling defensive, Jenn said, "I never drank because I saw Miranda come home a few times and spend the night on the floor in the bathroom. It seemed like a stupid way to have fun."

Trace picked up his coffee and took a sip. "Seems to me Kelly is a lot like Miranda."

Jenn nodded, glad to move the conversation back to Kelly. "More than either of them will admit."

Trace poured himself more coffee. "Want some?"

Jenn glanced at the clock on the stove and shook her head. "I may be able to get a couple of hours of sleep yet. Tell me where you found her."

"The Simons'. Parents are out of town. Went to

Europe for two weeks to celebrate their twentieth wedding anniversary, according to their boys."

Jenn frowned, trying to place the family's name.

"I think they moved here about four years ago. They bought the Bradford place, out on Pond Road. They left their sixteen- and seventeen-year-old sons home alone."

Jenn shook her head. "What were they thinking?"

"I think that will be their reaction when they see the house. The place is trashed. This is apparently not the first party the boys have had since their parents left."

"So it's bad?"

"For starters they had a leaky beer keg on the hardwood floor in the entryway."

Jenn winced. The floor would probably have to be replaced. "Is Kelly in trouble?"

He raised an eyebrow. "You mean from me?"

Jenn nodded.

Trace shook his head. "No. There must have been forty kids there. Word will get around and each parent will have to decide what to do about their own child."

Trace was right. Word would get around. Jenn rubbed tiredly at her eyes. She would have to tell Miranda first thing tomorrow before someone else did. That was one of the things she disliked about small-town living.

"It's my fault." She felt tears of frustration and self-recrimination well up. She'd failed to supervise the girl properly. She should have known.

"No, it's not." He tipped her chin up with his hand. "Hey. What's this?"

She sucked in a shuddering breath, afraid if she said anything she'd burst into tears.

Suddenly she found herself in the circle of his strong arms, being held against his broad warm chest. For the life of her she couldn't have said which one of them had moved.

"Jenn, let it go. You can't control everything."

But she had to try. It was the only way she knew to run her life. To keep the people she loved safe.

Oh, she thought as she felt the strength of his arms around her, this is a dangerous place to be. In spite of her warning, she laid her head against him and felt the steady beat of his heart. She told herself to pull away, but he must have read her thoughts, because his arms tightened just the tiniest bit.

For the first time in hours she felt safe. A minute, she thought, I'll just stay here a minute. She sighed and settled against him.

What could a minute hurt?

Chapter Seven

Trace held Jenn against his chest. She felt so right there.

He rested his cheek against her temple. How he had missed this woman. Until this moment he hadn't realized how much. He'd been so angry for so long he'd forgotten how right she felt in his arms.

A bit of his anger melted away, but there was too much distance between them for a moment like this to make much difference. He told himself the embrace was temporary, and meant nothing to her.

But his body was sending him a completely different message. The urge to coax her upstairs and into her bed hit him like an unexpected ocean wave, the kind that knocks you down and spins you around until you don't know which way is up.

Don't be a fool, he thought. He'd comforted enough people in his line of work to know how needy people became in the aftermath of a crisis.

She'd proven eight years ago how little she had wanted him in her life, and he'd be well served to remember the tough lessons he'd learned.

Trace stiffened his resolve and let his arms drop. When she didn't move, he set her away from him.

He felt her shiver as he let go of her.

He stepped back and forced himself to look down at her averted face. "You need to get some rest so you can deal with Kelly."

Jenn looked at him, her face unreadable, then she fixed her gaze on a spot just past his left shoulder. "I'm going to have to think about what her punishment should be. Maybe I'll lock her in her room and feed her bread and water until school starts."

He laughed, and didn't know whether to be relieved or sad. Once again they were polite acquaintances.

"Tomorrow, when you talk to her, remember what it was like to be a teenager."

"I never did anything like that as a teenager." As she spoke, she got a funny look on her face.

Trace knew what she was thinking. He remembered those nights as if they'd happened yesterday. She had been older than Kelly, and she hadn't gotten drunk, but she *had* snuck out of her bedroom late at night on more than one occasion.

To meet him.

The awkwardness was back, like a live thing between them.

Finally Jenn shifted and took a step away from him. "Thanks for everything. I appreciate all your help."

"No problem. I need to get going and you need some sleep."

He went to the front door, surprised that Jenn followed him out to his car.

"Trace, did Kelly have a purse with her when you found her?" Jenn's hair shimmered in the faint moonlight as if she was gilded in silver.

Trace ignored how appealing she looked and thought back to when he had spotted Kelly at the party.

"I don't know." In all the confusion, he didn't remember a purse.

He opened the driver's side door and the overhead light came on. There, partway under the backseat, was a small handbag covered with little squiggles.

"Found it." He dropped the heavy bag into Jenn's hand.

"Trace, thanks again. For everything." Her chin quivered.

He felt himself unraveling at the sight of her distress. He needed to leave, now, before he did something incredibly stupid.

"Hey. Go back inside and get some sleep," he said in a gruff voice. He would have taken a step back, but he was already up against the open car door.

"Can we at least be friends?" A big tear rolled down her cheek.

He'd never seen her cry. When she was upset or angry, she used to shut him out, not show a lot of emotion.

"Jenn, honey, we'll always be friends." He said the words, but they had a hollow ring.

He didn't feel like her friend. Friends didn't avoid each other for eight years then think about having sex the moment they met again. That wasn't friendship— it was something else entirely, and he wasn't going to go there.

He looked down at her.

Friends?

Hell, technically she was still his wife.

She gave him a watery smile, put her hands on his shoulders. The little purse smacked against his arm as she reached up to kiss him on the cheek.

He already knew how soft and warm she was from holding her in the kitchen. He caught the scent of flowers from her hair, and all rational thought left his brain. He slid his arms around her and pulled her against him, inhaling her scent. He didn't want to kiss her like a friend—he wanted to kiss her like a husband.

He turned his head just enough so he could cover her mouth with his. She froze for a moment, but instead of pushing away, she melted into him.

He felt the purse slip out of her hand, just the way his self-control was slipping away from him. His brain was yelling at him to stop, but his body was telling him something much different. He leaned into the kiss and relearned the feel of her.

She sighed into his mouth, and a bolt of potent lust hit him hard. He wanted to pin her against the side of his car, but she stiffened and pulled back.

Thank goodness one of them had some sense, he thought. Reluctantly, every fiber in him screaming for her, he let go of her. She took a step back, and then another, until she was out of his reach.

There was enough moonlight for him to see the confused look on her face.

That had been a truly stupid move on his part, on so many levels. She was exhausted and overwhelmed and he'd taken advantage of a simple kiss on the cheek. He knew Jenn well enough to know that when she had time to think, she wasn't going to be happy about what had just happened.

That was the way her mind worked. He was sure kissing him hadn't been part of her plans.

"I didn't mean that to happen," Jenn said.

Trace decided to go for humor. "Well, what can I say? You just can't resist a hottie."

Jenn laughed, and he saw her relax a bit.

He needed to go, before he grabbed her back into his arms. "Go inside, lock the door and go to bed." He made himself stand right where he was. It took a great deal of willpower.

She nodded and quickly scooped the purse off the ground. She walked away with a small backward wave of her hand.

"Idiot," he said to himself as he slid into the driver's seat.

He waited until the front door had closed behind her, then he pulled out of the drive.

He drove to his office through the deserted streets of Blossom, wondering if he'd lost his mind.

Kissing Jenn had been a monumental mistake.

She was going back to Dallas at the end of the summer. Some time between now and then she would make sure their marriage was annulled.

Did he want a repeat of what had happened eight years ago? Hardly. It was painfully obvious he still wasn't over the first time she'd walked out on him.

Pulling into his parking place behind the courthouse, he killed the engine and pushed thoughts of Jenn from his mind. There was still enough time to get some paperwork done before his deputies came off nightshift.

He unlocked the back door of the building. There was something leaning against the wall by the door to the sheriff's offices. On the floor stood a miniature statue of a jockey. The lawn ornament was handcuffed to the doorknob with a pair of plastic handcuffs.

Trace rubbed one hand over the tense muscles in his neck. Unless he was mistaken, the last time he had seen this particular piece of sculpture it had been in front of Bitsy Dupres's house. He shook his head and released the handcuffs. Wasn't this great. He picked up the heavy little statue by its outstretched arm and hauled it into his office.

Not even dawn yet and the day was off to a rip-roaring start.

Head spinning, Jenn let herself into the house and leaned against the door, listening to the sound of Trace's car pulling away.

She put her fingers to her lips. She could still feel his mouth on hers. She put her hand over her pounding heart. Only Trace had ever been able to get her so riled up.

She was too tired to think tonight. All she wanted was to put her head down and sleep.

On legs that felt like lead, she went upstairs and stopped to check on her niece. Kelly was in her bed, curled on her side in a fetal position. Jenn went into the bathroom, got the plastic wastebasket and put it beside the bed.

After turning off her niece's cell phone, she put Kelly's purse on the shelf in the closet in the guest room where she and Zack were sleeping. Then she went to bed herself, and fell asleep almost immediately.

Her dreams were colorful, to say the least, and every single one starred Trace.

Jenn woke up with the sun shining through her bedroom windows. She needed to pick up Zack and his friend for day camp. She showered and put on shorts and a blouse, then made her way to the kitchen.

The coffeepot was still on, and the smell of stale

coffee brought back memories of last night with a vengeance.

She could make up all kinds of excuses as to why she'd let Trace kiss her, but the fact was she'd enjoyed it. And she couldn't let it happen again.

She rinsed out the coffee carafe and started a fresh pot, needing the caffeine to get Trace off her mind and clear her head. She watched the coffee drip, feeling totally unprepared for everything she had to deal with today.

First things first. She'd get Kelly up and make her eat breakfast. Jenn smiled. That in itself would probably be a huge punishment, given how the girl was going to be feeling. Jenn could gauge Kelly's memory of last night's events and work from there. Then she'd haul Kelly to the fair to take care of her pig.

Okay, she thought as she measured out pancake mix. She could deal with Kelly.

Her hands stilled over the mixing bowl. What about Trace?

Last night had been all about overwrought emotions and out-of-control feelings. The kiss had been nothing but a reaction to a difficult situation. She'd meant what she'd said. She wanted Trace to be a friend, of sorts. She'd be running into him for the rest of her visit and it would be less awkward if they could put the past away and act like rational adults.

Oh, yeah, a little voice in her head mocked her. Just like last night, plastered against him and kissing him as if you wanted to drag him straight to bed.

She slammed the griddle down on the stove, hoping the noise would drown out her thoughts.

Friends, she told herself firmly. Nothing more.

They had both moved on with their lives years ago. They were wrong for each other. Trace was planted firmly in Blossom and she was going back to Dallas. She liked order and plans. Trace was too spontaneous.

He'd proven that by talking her into running away and getting married. If she'd let herself think about it all those years ago, she would have realized it was a bad plan.

She shook off the thought and went upstairs to wake her niece.

She stood in the doorway and watched the sleeping girl. Kelly looked like a child, curled up in bed. Jenn felt an evil satisfaction at what she was about to do. She walked to east-facing window and yanked up the shade. Sunshine poured into the room.

"Good morning!"

Kelly groaned and rolled to face the wall.

Jenn shook her. "Time to get up," she said in a loud, cheerful voice.

Kelly moaned and pulled the covers over her head.

"Come on, Kelly. I'm making pancakes," Jenn said, keeping her tone light.

An unintelligible mutter emerged from under the covers.

"Now, Kelly. We have to leave in a few minutes to pick up Zack." Jenn left the room and headed back downstairs.

She heated up the griddle and made the first batch of pancakes, which she loaded onto a plate and placed on the table for Kelly. She'd turned back to the stove when she heard her niece come into the kitchen.

"Sit down and eat. We need to get going." Jenn glanced over her shoulder and noted that Kelly's face still looked a little green.

Kelly slid into her chair without looking at Jenn and picked up her fork as Jenn put a helping of pancakes on her own plate and carried it to the table. Kelly stared at her plate, her fork suspended in the air. She shot Jenn a quick puzzled look, then gingerly took a bite of breakfast. It was all Jenn needed to decide Kelly did not remember getting home last night.

Jenn wouldn't say a word for now. She'd leave Kelly's purse and cell phone on the shelf in her closet and let the child think about what had happened. They would talk tonight, after Jenn had broken the news about last night's escapade to Miranda.

"Come on, Kelly. Eat up. You need to go take care of Petunia." Jenn took another big bite of pancakes.

She watched the suffering teenager out of the corner of her eye and hoped with shameless glee that the pig's pen was extra nasty today.

Chapter Eight

Jenn watched Kelly replace the straw in Petunia's pen. The girl moved so carefully it looked as if she was afraid her head might roll off her shoulders.

So far Kelly hadn't said a word about last night, and she hadn't mentioned her missing purse or cell phone.

In fact, she had said very little, period.

She kept glancing at Jenn with a puzzled look on her face, then quickly looking away when Jenn caught her eye.

Jenn planned to leave things undiscussed for the moment. It would do Kelly good to ponder what had happened last night and what was going to happen today.

Several of Kelly's friends had stopped by to say

hello. Jenn kept her expression pleasant and let them wonder.

They probably thought they were being subtle, but Jenn had a very good idea of who had been at the party last night by their body language.

The morning had put Kelly in a state of agony and very much improved Jenn's disposition.

When she was sure Kelly would survive the ordeal of caring for the pig and her litter, she said, "I'm going to check on Zack at day camp. I'll be back for you in an hour or so, and we'll have lunch. Don't forget we're signed up to help judge pies and cakes."

Kelly's face twisted in a sour expression and she started to nod, then stopped abruptly, as if the motion caused her pain.

Jenn hid her smile. She had stopped by the fair offices this morning while Kelly fed her pig and signed the two of them up for every activity she could find. She told herself she didn't want Kelly to have too much spare time, but she also realized the more time she spent at the fairgrounds, the more chances she'd have to run into Trace.

She hadn't forgotten how it had felt to be in his arms last night. She knew she was playing with fire, and it wasn't like her to be rash, but she couldn't seem to avoid temptation when it came to Trace.

Jenn felt another perverse stab of glee as she put the straps of her purse over her shoulder and fired her parting shot. "Have you tried the deep-fried Twinkies yet? We could get some after lunch." With that she headed for the parking lot.

She had no doubt that as soon as she was gone Kelly's friends would come back and they would all compare notes. Kelly would soon have the gaps in her memory at least partially filled in. This afternoon she and Kelly would talk, after Jenn had told Miranda what had happened.

Before driving to the day camp, Jenn stopped at the hospital. The smell of disinfectant and the sight of the white tile floors and mint-green walls brought her the usual wave of sadness.

Both her mother and father had died in this hospital. Miranda's first husband, whom Jenn had adored, had died here, too, and this is where she'd come when she'd miscarried Trace's baby.

As the soles of her sandals squeaked along the polished floors she ruthlessly pushed the sad memories out of her mind. Miranda would have a happy outcome. Jenn refused to consider any other possibility.

She paused outside her sister's room and took a deep breath. She hoped they hadn't moved anyone else into Miranda's room. She didn't want to air dirty laundry in front of a stranger. She stopped, her hand on the door. This was the second time in as many days that she'd thought like her mother.

Could Trace be right? Did Jenn have control issues, like her mother? Jenn rubbed the ache in her forehead above her eyes. It was something she would have to think about. Later.

Jenn pushed open the door and found Miranda propped up in bed watching TV.

Her sister broke into a big smile. "Hey, Jenn. I didn't expect to see you until this afternoon."

To Jenn's relief, Miranda looked rested and refreshed. "Zack's at day camp and Kelly is taking care of her pig, so I thought I'd sneak away and see how you're doing."

"No contractions, and my blood pressure is down."

Jenn nodded as she pulled up a chair. "Good news. But hold onto your handrails. That may change."

Miranda shot her a suspicious look. "What happened? Did you have a talk with Trace about the annulment?"

She felt her face heat up at the mention of his name. No, they hadn't talked much, but he had kissed her and her brain had turned to mush.

Miranda grinned and gestured to the chair. "Come tell your big sister all about it."

"It's about Trace." Well, not the part she was going to tell Miranda. She sat down. "Kelly snuck out and went to a party last night. Trace found her for me and brought her home a little under the weather."

Miranda's expression changed to worry. "She catch a bug?"

Jenn shook her head. "No. She caught too many beers."

Miranda pushed herself up on her pillows. "Oh, Lordy. She's just a child."

"Actually, I remember you coming home in about

the same condition at about the same age," Jenn said drily.

"That was different!" Miranda said defensively.

Jenn just raised an eyebrow and waited.

"Okay, okay," Miranda said, sounding chagrined. "You didn't tell her that, did you?"

"Of course not! I'm not going to tell her any of the stuff you used to do," she said, grinning at her sister.

Miranda looked relieved as she huffed out a reluctant laugh and settled back against the pillows. "So what happened?"

Jenn related what she knew, and how she had handled the situation so far.

Miranda shook her head. "I had forgotten how diabolical you really are."

Jenn shrugged, pleased that her sister seemed to be taking the news as well as she was. "My first impulse was to yell at her and ground her for the rest of her life, but there has been a lot of satisfaction in watching her suffer."

Miranda nodded. "It's been a tough year for her. Not that that's an excuse!"

"What do you want me to do?" Jenn needed Miranda to make the final decision on her daughter's punishment.

"Keeping her purse and cell phone is brilliant. Don't let her know you have it for a few days."

Jenn nodded her head in mock humility. "Thank you."

Miranda considered the situation for a moment. "I could yell at her when she comes in this afternoon."

Jenn thought about that. "How did you feel when Mom yelled at you?"

Miranda shook her head and looked chagrined. "Like I wanted to go and do it all over again just to show her I could."

Jenn nodded, remembering the arguments Miranda and her mother used to have. "How about I have a little heart-to-heart with her when the time is right?"

Miranda gave her a grateful look. "That would probably be better. She might listen to you."

Jenn glanced at her watch. "She doesn't even have to know you know."

Miranda nodded. "Thank Trace for me, will you?" she said as Jenn stood to bid her sister goodbye.

"I will," Jenn said, annoyed that the excuse to see him made her heart beat faster. She was thinking like a teenager. How foolish could she get?

The answer to that question scared the daylights out of her.

She wished she did have too much self-control, she thought. She could use some of it now.

Trace stood on Bitsy Dupres's porch and watched her welcome her lawn jockey back as if it had been a kidnapped child. She dabbed at her eyes with a pink handkerchief while she stroked the chipped paint on the statue's head.

"Oh, Sheriff, how can I thank you?"

Trace struggled to hide his smile. "No thanks necessary, Bitsy." At least she wasn't trying to blame the theft on the carnival folks.

He'd managed to get the statue back to her before she'd even noticed it was missing, unlike the four calls he'd received about statues this morning.

Seems the kids who lived around Blossom had been busy last night. The petty vandalism probably had occurred on the way to or from the party where he'd found Kelly.

Three of the lawn ornaments had been recovered. He'd found a pair of white plaster geese perched on the edge of the fountain in front of a bank in a neighboring town.

The ugliest cement elf he'd ever laid eyes on, with wild stringy hair, had been left at the back door to the Cut and Curl. A string around the statue's wrist had held a note begging for a complete makeover. It amazed him that the owner even wanted it back.

Given what he usually dealt with where teenagers were concerned, he considered the missing yard statues pretty benign. Unfortunately the kids were targeting the members of the Committee for Moral Behavior.

The victims saw the incidents as another indicator that the younger generation was out of control. Their dire predictions had the perpetrators "going to hell" and "on the road to major crime." Trace was sure the vandalism would end just as soon as school started.

After refusing an offer of breakfast from Bitsy, he headed to the fairgrounds. When Jason Strong called, Trace pulled to the side of the road to answer his cell phone. "Hey, Jason. What can I do for you?"

He heard his friend's deep laugh. "I hate to bother you during the current crime spree, but I wondered if you had assigned anyone to traffic control after the concert?"

"Yup. Got two extra deputies assigned." A popular local country singer was coming to Blossom to perform and they were expecting a big crowd at the fair on Saturday night.

"Good. I heard you escorted Miranda's daughter home last night."

Trace grimaced. "I did." News certainly traveled fast in Blossom. He hoped if Jenn had managed to speak to Miranda before the gossip began. "The Simons left their teenagers home alone. We broke up the party around 3:00 a.m."

"Much damage?"

Trace said, "Enough that those boys probably won't be left alone for the rest of their natural lives."

Jason laughed again. "I'm keeping Rikki at home until she's thirty."

Trace joined his friend in a laugh. Jason's precocious daughter was nearly three. "That's a long time, buddy. Might cut in to your social life."

Jason made a noncommittal sound. "Speaking of social life, I hear you're seeing Jenn?"

Trace winced. He knew the gossips put the two of

them together, simply because they were both single and had dated in high school. He didn't even want to think about what they would say if they had any inkling he and Jenn had been married—and still were.

"Trace?"

"Yeah. I'm here." He didn't answer Jason's question.

"Thought you might want to know. Jenn was in the fair office this morning. She signed herself and Kelly up for every activity still open."

Trace digested that tidbit of information, then said, "Hey, Jason?"

"Yeah?"

"She sign up for anything this afternoon?"

He heard papers rustling. "Yeah."

"Put me down, too."

"Sure thing, buddy." Jason laughed as he hung up.

Ever since Trace had seen Jenn in the pigpen he'd been thinking of asking her to help him with the investigation of the land swindle. Her experience in forensic accounting could prove invaluable, and the sheriff's department was having trouble coming up with the extra money to hire someone. He hoped she'd do it, as a favor for him, and he told himself that was the only reason he wanted to see her.

Jason was gone by the time Trace parked behind the fair security office, so he checked the judges' sign-up sheets and noted he was judging pies and cakes in half an hour. He would count the judging as his lunch break, since with today's schedule he wasn't likely to get time to eat.

He leaned against the desk and rubbed the back of his neck. The short night was catching up with him. And so was his foolish behavior. Why had he arranged his free time so he could spend it with her? What had he been thinking? There wasn't a future for them. Too much water under their particular bridge.

She'd made her feelings very clear. She was going through with the annulment. In a few weeks she'd be headed back home to Dallas. And when Jenn made plans, she stuck to them.

He was an idiot, staring at her name above his on a list and looking forward to seeing her again. It made no sense. He felt happier than he had in a long time.

He couldn't seem to help himself.

He never could when Jenn was involved.

Chapter Nine

Waiting for the greased-pig race to start, Jenn sat at the judge's table, her eyes covered by sunglasses. Trace stood with the other boys and men in the arena below. In spite of the heat, he wore jeans and a long-sleeved plaid shirt. He kept glancing in her direction, and she had to fight to keep the smirk off her face. He'd always been a good sport.

He'd signed himself up as a judge for this event, but after suffering through the baking contest she'd crossed his name out and put him down as a participant. The thought of sitting side by side for another competition was too appealing.

She grinned and waved at him, and he waved back.

He wanted her to help in an investigation, and she'd been tempted to accept the challenge. She loved that kind of work, but more than that, he knew she'd enjoy spending time with Trace. So she'd turned him down.

Trace was right. She struggled with control issues. When she was around him, she didn't have enough for her peace of mind.

Zack turned around in his seat just in front of the judging table and smiled at her. Day camp was over, and he was spending time with her and Kelly, who had opted out of this event to be with her pig.

He was being a good sport about attending the competitions, but all he wanted to do was go on the rides. So far she'd discouraged him.

She did *not* want to go on the Tilt-a-Whirl or any other ride on the midway. She didn't enjoy the wild spins and dizzy feelings the rides gave her. She didn't want to be strapped into some contraption that she couldn't control, nor would she feel comfortable watching her son climb on by himself

Zack waved to get her attention and then pointed at Trace. She nodded and smiled. Zack had become curious about Trace over the past few days. She wasn't surprised. The boy had never really had a man pay as much attention to him as Trace did. Trace had even learned some basic signing. When Jenn's surprise had shown he'd just smiled and said you could learn anything on the Internet these days.

He was acting like a friend, nothing more. Hadn't she said she wanted just that? Friendship?

Her head told her that friendship *was* what she

wanted, but her heart and body were sending her other messages. Messages she carefully squashed every time they arrived.

The announcer told the participants to get ready. The men and boys milled around, waiting for the pigs to be released.

Jenn glanced down at the short list of rules. This was one event that was easy to judge. There were four age groups and four pigs. Catch and hold on to a pig and the pig was yours.

An air horn sounded and the gates at the far end of the arena flew open. Four half-grown pigs, caked with what looked like white vegetable shortening, were chased, squealing, into the ring. Pandemonium erupted as the men and boys pounded after the speedy little porkers. Dirt and dust rose in a cloud that partially obscured the activity, but that didn't stop the crowd from yelling and cheering the men on.

The first pig was caught by a boy about Kelly's age. The others in his category congratulated him and went to stand against the fence. The next two pigs were caught at about the same time. There was such a jumble of men that at first Jenn couldn't figure out who actually had possession of the animals.

When everyone got themselves untangled, Trace was one of the winners. He held the furious animal trapped against his chest, and from his hair to his boots he was covered in dust and dirt and bits of hay.

He looked at the stands, right at her, and held up his index finger.

Jenn covered her mouth with her hand and smiled. She'd seen Trace and Jason and Blake Gray Feather use that signal among themselves.

He was telling her she owed him.

She remembered her duties as judge and pulled her gaze away from Trace to watch the last group, the youngest, corner and catch the pig. It was a group effort. She couldn't tell who had actually caught the animal, but they all seemed satisfied that the smallest boy in the group should take custody of the pig.

Jenn glanced over at Trace again, wondering what he was going to do with a pig, and saw him handing it off to one of the boys who had competed.

How like Trace.

She knew the boy's family. He was a little younger than Kelly, and for several generations his folks had farmed a worn-out tract of land near Denton Pond. That piglet meant the family would have meat this winter. Her heart trembled with emotion. Trace was a truly fine man. Somehow over the years, in her need to bury her feelings, she'd forgotten that about him.

Zack signed that he wanted to congratulate Trace. Jenn was hesitant, given the fact that she had entered him without his permission. There was no way she could explain that to her son, though, so she followed him out of the stands.

They caught up with Trace at the entrance to the arena, where he stood talking to some of the other men. The only part of him that wasn't filthy was his hat, which he hadn't worn into the ring. The front of his shirt was crusted with blobs of shortening caked with dirt and straw. Jenn bit the inside of her lip to keep from laughing.

He spotted them, and his mouth quirked up in a little smile. "Hey, Zack. Jenn."

Zack signed his congratulations to Trace.

"Thanks, Zack. Couple of years and you'll be old enough to join in."

The expression on her son's face let Jenn know he was looking forward to it.

Could she come back to Blossom for the summer in the future? Jenn didn't know. She loved visiting Miranda, and Zack was having the time of his life, but what if she came back and found Trace had fallen for someone? It was bound to happen. He was the best-looking single man in Blossom.

She shook her head at her foolishness as she watched him talk to her son.

His gaze shifted to her face and he caught her looking at him. She tried to look away, but there was something in his eyes that held her—that twinkle, that knowing look she remembered so well. Her whole body began to hum. He used to look at her like that when he knew they would be alone later, when he knew they'd make love.

He took a step forward. "I just want to thank you for *nudging* me into this."

The silky tone of his voice as he moved toward her had her face heating up and put her on guard. She stepped back to get out of his range. Trace's hand shot out and locked on her wrist, then he pulled her into a bear hug. She squealed, sounding a lot like one of the piglets.

Everyone around them laughed. Mortified at the sounds she was making, she worked her hands up to his chest to give him a shove. He let go of her easily enough, but the damage was done. Her striped cotton blouse was smeared with dirt and grease and her white shorts were hopelessly smudged.

Zack was laughing like a loon.

She looked down at herself and shook her head. She supposed she'd had that hug coming. The trouble was, she wanted more.

When she glanced up at Trace, he was grinning, his teeth very white against his dirty face. "Even?"

She tried to look angry, but felt the smile break over her face. Reluctantly she said, "I suppose."

"Good," he said, and grabbed her again.

This time he planted a kiss on her mouth that had her forgetting all about the state of his clothes and who was watching.

He'd always been a great kisser. Hazily, as his lips did a very thorough job on her mouth, she realized he was even better now. A stab of jealousy brought her to her senses. She broke the kiss and stepped back.

She gave herself a mental shake. What did she have to be jealous of? Did she think he'd lived like a monk for the past eight years? She should be more worried about the fact that half of Blossom had just seen him kissing her.

Trace let go of her and stood smiling, one eyebrow raised. "Now I guess you owe me."

She wasn't going to touch that comment with a ten-foot pole. Her son, along with half the town, had witnessed the whole exchange. Zack had a disgusted look on his face, which didn't surprise Jenn in the least. He was at the stage where he thought kissing of any kind was yucky.

As her heartbeat returned to normal, Jenn glanced at her watch, then down at her filthy clothes. "I have just enough time to go home and change before the quilt judging."

Embarrassed by the breathless tone of her voice, she refused to look at Trace as she grabbed Zack by the hand and headed for her car.

Trace's deep chuckle followed her. "I'm looking forward to it."

Oh great, she thought, and kept on walking. He wasn't going to leave her alone.

A little shiver of anticipation worked its way down her spine.

Trace stripped off his shirt and tossed it onto the floor of his truck. He was still filthy, but at least he didn't have any grease on his butt. He jammed his truck into Drive and headed toward his house.

He'd been a good sport about the greased-pig contest, and so had Jenn about the hug that had followed. He *had* owed her that.

The kiss was something else entirely.

What the heck had made him think *that* was a good idea?

Half the town had been around to see that kiss, including Billy Ray Wilkens. Billy Ray, who while they were waiting for the contest to start had commented on what a hot number Jenn was. Trace had felt the need to brand her, just so Billy Ray knew.

Knew *what?* Trace yelled at himself. That he and Jenn had gone together when she was still in high school?

That they were married?

And just why did *that* thought keep popping into his head?

Once at his house, he stuffed his clothes into the washer and headed to the shower.

Why couldn't he be smart about her? There were plenty of women in Texas.

But only one of them was Jenn, he thought sadly as he wiped soapy foam off his face.

His hands stilled. Somewhere during the past few days his anger at her over leaving eight years ago had disappeared.

When had that happened?

The night he'd brought Kelly home.

He'd begun to see past his hurt and realize how hard it must have been for Jenn. How frightened and alone she'd been, with him in San Antonio. She'd tried to forget everything that had happened. He suspected it hadn't worked any better for her than it had for him.

So where did that leave them?

Friends?

Not likely, he thought as he rinsed off. He *never* fantasized about his friends being naked in his bed.

He turned off the water and reached for a towel. So what were they? How would he define the relationship? More than friends.

And still married. Jenn hadn't filled the papers yet, even though she'd seemed adamant a few days ago.

But that was before they'd kissed—twice.

Why not coax her into his bed? She was going to be here for the rest of the summer.

They were both adults. And they deserved to know what it might have been like if they'd stayed together.

First he'd talk her into helping him investigate the swindle. That would guarantee more time together. Then he'd tempt her into his bed.

Finally he had a plan. And one he liked, he thought happily. But before he could get back to the fair— and Jenn—he drove to his office to check in.

When he walked in, Henrie said, "Sheriff, I was about to call you." She nodded her head at the waiting area. "Miss Webster would like a minute."

Trace nodded and smiled at the woman as she got slowly to her feet. Beulah Webster. She'd recently retired from teaching at the elementary school.

Trace held the door for her. "Come on back to my office, Miss Webster."

The gray-haired woman passed him, clutching a purse in one hand and a handkerchief in the other.

She wore a floral print dress and smelled like baby powder.

Trace seated her in the chair across from his desk and then took his seat, glancing quickly at the clock on his desk and hoping this wasn't going to take long. He needed to judge quilts. With Jenn.

He refrained from rolling his eyes at his own stupidity.

"What can I do for you Miss Webster?" he asked.

"It's about my mother." She dabbed at her lips with the handkerchief. "I've been cleaning out Mother's things, to move her into my home, you know. And I came across some papers. I fear my mother has been the victim of a flimflam man."

Trace hid his smile at her old-fashioned phrase and listened as Beulah Webster told him a story he'd heard a number of times over the past two years. The land swindle—con artists had bilked quite a few county residents out of a lot of money. He wondered how many other victims were out there, too embarrassed to report the crime.

When Miss Webster stopped talking and dabbed tearfully at her eyes, Trace asked, "Will your mother come in and sign a complaint?"

Beulah Webster shook her head sadly. "I don't think so. She's mortified by being taken in, you see."

Trace nodded sympathetically. "I understand. Would it help her to know that she's not alone? Quite a number of people have signed complaints already."

Miss Webster's hand fluttered near her ample flowered bosom. "Oh, I was afraid of that."

"Your instincts are good. Con artists rarely target just one person. Would it help if I talked to your mother?"

Miss Webster shook her head stood up to leave. "Let me try again. She may feel differently if she knows there were others."

Trace got to his feet. "Let her know how important it is, Miss Webster. The more information we get, the better chance we have to catch the people who did this."

"Thank you, Sheriff. I'll try." She headed for the door and waved him back. "No need to show me out. I'm going to have a chat with Henrietta before I leave."

He stood by his desk, frustrated that he hadn't been able to track down the people who had preyed on the residents of Blossom County.

He didn't have the expertise to look into the financial end of the scheme, and the county had promised to send him a team of accountants, but with all the budget cuts, it hadn't happened yet.

He really needed Jenn's help.

Yup, he thought, it was good to have a plan.

Chapter Ten

Jenn walked with Zack into the pig barn to get Kelly for the quilt judging. Her niece was talking to a sandy-haired boy Jenn didn't recognize.

Immediately Jenn stiffened with suspicion. The boy looked at least sixteen. Had he been the one to drive Kelly to the party?

Kelly had been contrite about her behavior, but she had stubbornly refused to name any of her friends or tell Jenn how she had gotten across town to the Simon house that night.

Jenn understood the teenagers' unwritten law: you never ratted on your friends. Still, she worried about Kelly hanging out with someone who was willing to pick her up in the middle of the night.

Kelly spotted Jenn and blushed.

"Hey, Kelly," Jenn looked pointedly at the boy.

Kelly smiled, the first happy expression Jenn had seen on the girl's face in days.

"Hey, Aunt Jenn." She hesitated a moment and glanced shyly at the tall young man standing beside her. "This is Ryan."

"Ryan, nice to meet you." She put her hand on Zack's head. "This is my son, Zack."

"Nice to meet you, too, Mrs.—"

"It's Miss. Miss Williams. What's your last name?"

"Stone."

Jenn must have looked puzzled as she searched her memory for a family named Stone, because Ryan supplied, "We just moved to Blossom on Saturday."

Okay, so he wasn't the one who'd taken Kelly to the party. That was a point in his favor.

"From where?" Jenn could see Kelly starting to fidget, and she knew her niece was embarrassed by Jenn's questions.

"Near Houston. My dad wants to live in the country." He looked as if he wasn't at all sure his dad hadn't lost his mind.

"Ryan thinks he might want to join 4H and raise a pig," Kelly said.

Jenn glanced into the pen, where Petunia's piglets were scattered around like pieces of pink cordwood, sleeping and snoring with little piggy grunts.

"Well," she said in a dry tone, "I know where you can get one."

Ryan laughed.

"Kelly, are you finished here? We need to get over to the quilt judging."

Kelly snuck a glance at Ryan. "I'm done."

Ryan stuck his hands into his pockets and gave Kelly a shy look. "Will you be here tomorrow?"

Kelly sighed. "I'll be here every day until the final judging."

He shrugged. "Okay, then. I guess I'll see you tomorrow."

Kelly matched his casual shrug, as if she really didn't care. "Okay."

Ryan turned to go, and Jenn saw Kelly's face change as she watched him walk away. The expression on her niece's face brought back a stab of memory so sharp and sweet Jenn closed her eyes for a moment. How many times had she looked at Trace that way?

"Aunt Jenn?"

Jenn opened her eyes. "Yes?"

"Do you think he's cute?" Kelly asked on a sigh.

Jenn nodded. "Oh, yes, sweetheart, he's definitely cute."

The fortune-teller's words predicting love for Kelly echoed in Jenn's head. One love will last all your life. The other will become a pleasant memory. Well, time would tell.

When they got to the building where the quilts were being judged, Jenn put her hand on Zack's shoulder to settle him down. Poor kid. He'd been so good tagging along while Jenn kept Kelly busy, but she knew he was reaching his limit. She just hoped he'd make it through this final event.

The list of judging criteria was four pages long and the woman in charge was reciting a lengthy list of instructions.

Suddenly her spine tingled. She turned her head and caught sight of Trace coming through the door. He'd showered and changed into his uniform, and he looked absolutely delicious.

He smiled at her, and she struggled against an expression much like the one now decorating her niece's features. She told herself for the hundredth time that day not to be a fool. There was already enough gossip after that very public kiss.

Luckily, before she did something she might regret, the woman in charge of the judging stepped into Trace's path.

She waved a finger at him. "Sheriff, I don't know exactly why you're here."

Trace smiled down at the tightly wound little woman. "I'm here going to help with the judging."

He glanced over at Jenn and she was pretty sure he winked at her. She held her clipboard against her chest and wondered how far his charm would get him.

"You signed your name at the bottom of the page! There was not even a line with a number for your name. We have no more clipboards!" The woman's face was turning an alarming shade of pink.

Trace put his hands up in a placating gesture. "I wouldn't want to inconvenience you."

The woman nodded, then hurried off to shake her finger at one of the judges who was touching a quilt.

Just then Zack raced over to Trace, signing furiously about the greased-pig contest.

Jenn closed the distance between them and translated what Zack had to say.

Trace patiently answered the boy's questions, speaking directly to Zack so he'd have a chance to read Trace's lips.

When Zack wound down, Trace leaned over to Jenn and nodded toward the quilt lady. In a quiet tone he said, "Remember Mrs. Nelson from high school?"

Jenn nodded. She certainly did remember that tyrant. Jenn had had home room with her for two years running.

He whispered in her ear. "I think they're sisters."

Jenn smiled, trying to ignore the shivers his low voice caused. "Mrs. Nelson didn't like boys. I don't think this woman likes *anyone.*"

Trace chuckled.

The sound went straight to her stomach, making it flutter in the most alarming way. Hoping to ignore that—and how good he smelled—Jenn said, "So I guess you aren't going to be a judge."

Trace shook his head. "Nope. No clipboard for me."

"You could have mine."

"I'm sure that's not allowed."

Jenn sighed. "I'm sure you're right."

Zack bumped against her, his arms crossed over

his chest. Jenn rubbed the top of his head. "I hope this doesn't take too long. Zack is about out of patience."

Trace glanced at Zack, then back at Jenn. "I'm going to head out and see Blake Gray Feather at the Tucker place. Why don't I take him with me?"

All kinds of reasons jumped into Jenn's head, none of them having to do with Trace's ability to supervise her son. "I don't know…" She was having a hard enough time resisting him. Now she'd be getting pressure from Zack, too.

"Jenn, why don't you let the boy decide. May I ask him?"

Jenn hesitated, unable to think of a believable excuse.

Her main objections had nothing to do with safety and everything to do with Trace being in her life. She was beginning to look forward to seeing him way too much.

She reminded herself she'd better call New Mexico first thing tomorrow. She'd been putting it off for far too long, and she didn't want to think about why.

But she knew Zack would love to go, so in spite of her fears, she said, "Okay.'

Trace squatted down, and in very simple words told Zack where he was going and asked if the boy wanted to go with him.

Zack nodded enthusiastically. Jenn quickly signed that he was to behave himself as he fairly danced with excitement.

Trace grabbed Zack's hand. "Where will you be after this?"

"I'm going to the hospital to see Miranda and then home."

Trace checked his watch. "I'll bring him back to Miranda's by suppertime."

"Okay. Keep a close eye on him. He's not used to being around animals."

He gave her a long, solemn look. "Trust me, Jenn."

"I do." She did trust him, with the most precious thing in her life, her son.

She wasn't concerned about Zack. It was her own heart she worried about.

Trace watched the excitement on Zack's little face and called himself all kinds of fool for bringing the kid out here.

It was going to be hard enough on Trace when Jenn left, and now he was starting to fall for her kid, too. In fact, he was dangerously close to falling in love with Jenn all over again. Now, wouldn't that be a monumentally stupid thing to do? He rubbed his hand over his chest and tightened his hold on the horse's bridle.

She was a pretty little mare, the gentlest, most predictable horse in the Tucker barn, a good horse for Zack's first ride. As far as Trace could determine, Zack had never been on a horse before. The kid might be deaf, but he had no trouble communicating.

"Hey, McCabe," Blake said from his perch on

the fence. "I understand you've been hanging around Jenn."

Trace turned the horse so Zack couldn't read Blake's lips. "Got to love the gossips in a small town."

Blake laughed. "Yeah. I was out at the Alibi a few nights ago and you two were topic number one. Breaking the hearts of single women all over Blossom."

Trace sent Blake a rude hand gesture behind his back and led Zack in another circle.

Trace checked the boy's feet in the shortened stirrups and the way he was holding the reins.

Blake shifted on the fence. "So, how are you doing?"

Trace wasn't sure how much Blake knew about what had happened eight years ago, but his friend had always been a keen observer. "I'm doing fine."

Blake made a gesture toward Zack. "This little guy belong to you?"

Trace looked at Zack then back at Blake. "Nope, but I wouldn't mind if he did." His answer surprised himself almost as much as it seemed to surprise Blake.

"I used to wonder what it would be like to have a girl as gone on me as Jenn was on you in high school." His voice had a wistful tone Trace had never heard from Blake.

Trace laughed. "But you know now."

Blake laughed with him and rubbed his hand along the leg of his jeans. "Yeah. I know now," he said, his voice filled with quiet awe.

Just then the screen door of the ranch house

smacked against the frame, and Trace saw Blake's fiancée, Cindy Tucker, headed toward them. She waved and called, "Hey, Trace."

Trace waved back. He watched Blake's face soften as his friend turned and vaulted off the fence. Blake met Cindy halfway across the yard, grabbed her and kissed her full on the mouth, then swung her around until her feet left the ground. A flash of light glinted off the ring on her left hand.

"Blake," Cindy laughed and pushed at his shoulders until he let her down.

Looking at him and smiling, she said, "What was that for?"

He gave her a tender look. "Just because, darlin', just because."

Cindy and Blake were planning a Christmas wedding.

Trace felt a jolt go through him, as if he'd been struck by lightning.

That's what he wanted. What he saw on Blake's face. He wanted complete happiness. And he was terribly afraid the only person who could give that to him was Jenn. The woman who was dead set on annulling their marriage and leaving him behind.

Chapter Eleven

Jenn heard the screen door slam, and Zack came bursting into the kitchen, grinning as if he'd just been given free rein in a toy store. His face was smeared with dirt, his clothes were dusty and his hands were downright filthy as he signed his excitement to Jenn.

"Whoa. Sounds like you had a great time, but let's talk after you've washed up." She pointed him to the sink in the utility room, then looked up to find Trace in the doorway.

Trace didn't look the worse for wear. In fact, he looked pretty terrific in his old jeans, boots and T-shirt. He must have changed at the Tuckers'.

Jenn swallowed and reminded herself that staring at him was not a good idea, on a lot of levels. "How is Blake?" she asked lightly. "And Cindy?"

Miranda had told her the two had gotten engaged.

"Good. Planning a Christmas wedding." He stared at her intently, as if he were trying to figure something out.

She looked away, uncomfortable with his scrutiny, and gestured to the utility room. "It seems he had a good time."

Trace pushed his big frame away from the door-jamb. "He took to the horse like a veteran. Not a bit scared."

Jenn didn't miss the hint of pride in Trace's voice. "Thank you for taking him out to see Blake," she said as she stirred the pot of spaghetti sauce.

Trace shrugged as if it had been no big deal. He moved to stand a few feet behind her. She could smell the outdoors on him—hay, saddle soap and a hint of horse. Familiar and way too pleasant.

"My pleasure." He leaned forward, sniffed at the spaghetti sauce and spoke into her ear. "How's Miranda doing?"

She shivered and tried to focus on his question. "Uh, medically she's doing fine, but the bed rest is driving her crazy." She wished he'd back up so she could think. "The doctors say if she can hold out for another week it'll be good."

He just said, "Hmm."

She could feel his eyes on her. Unsettled, she groped around for conversation. "Blake still riding rodeo?"

"He's thinking about retiring."

"Really?" Trace was still right behind her. Her body warmed up, disconcerting her. She groped for the thread of their conversation. "Will he help Tucker run the ranch?"

"I imagine," Trace said, and leaned forward, his chest against her back. He inhaled through his nose, and now she couldn't tell if he was sniffing the spaghetti sauce or her.

Impulsively she said, "Stay to supper?" Then she immediately wanted to suck the words back. She concentrated on the sauce, furiously rotating the big spoon.

Why had she done that? She'd promised herself that she would stay out of his way. Being with Trace brought up dangerous feelings she should be trying to avoid, but when he was close he totally muddled up her thought processes.

He didn't move. "Sure."

Silence descended between them, and seemed to hold them captive until Zack came back into the kitchen, his hands dripping. Jenn sidestepped away from the stove, reached for the towel on the counter and tossed it to her son.

She signed to him that Trace was staying for supper, and he asked if he could show Trace his room.

Jenn quickly tried to remember if she had left any personal items lying around in the room she and Zack shared. She was pretty sure she'd tidied up this morning. "Go ahead. Food will be ready in a few minutes."

She threw an apologetic glance at Trace as Zack raced out of the room. "He wants you to see his room. Hope you don't mind."

He studied her for a long moment before he replied, "I don't mind a bit."

Zack returned and grabbed Trace by the hand, dragging him out of the kitchen. Obviously he didn't think Trace was moving quickly enough.

As soon as they were out of sight she went into the downstairs bathroom to check her hair and put on lip gloss, all the while trying to convince herself she wasn't doing it for Trace.

Jenn set the table in the kitchen to the bass thump coming through the ceiling from Kelly's room. She drained the pasta, then carried the dishes to the table. When everything was ready she went to the bottom of the stairs, took a deep breath and called everyone down to eat.

Zack appeared immediately and Jenn could hear Kelly's and Trace's voices in the dining room. She realized this was the first time Kelly had been alone with him since he'd hauled her home from the party. Jenn couldn't hear the conversation, but from the tone it sounded as if Kelly was apologizing.

Jenn felt a swell of pride in her niece. It couldn't be easy for the teen.

The two of them walked into the kitchen and Jenn realized something about her niece was different.

Kelly had on makeup. It was subtle, but definitely there. Also, her hair was freshly washed and down around her shoulders instead of being in her usual ponytail. Add that to the low-rider jeans and the cropped tank top, and Kelly looked a lot older and more sophisticated.

Jenn's thoughts flashed to the boy who had been at the pigpen this afternoon. Was Kelly expecting him to stop by? She glanced over at Trace, who was busy loading his plate with pasta.

She'd acted the same way at Kelly's age, spending extra time on her hair and makeup if there had been any chance Trace would stop by. She missed the thrill of anticipation she'd felt when she'd dated Trace, the delicious waiting and wondering. Was there anything that felt as good as falling in love for the first time?

"Jenn, you okay?" Trace's voice brought her out of the past.

She shrugged. "Sure. I'm fine. A little tired." She reminded herself to stay away from those kinds of memories. It was too dangerous to go there.

When they finished eating, Jenn stood to take the dishes to the sink. But Trace pushed back his chair and took the plates out of her hand. "You cooked. Kelly and Zack and I will do the dishes."

Why did he always say the right thing? It made him so hard to resist. "Okay. I'll be out on the porch." Alone, she thought, trying to remember all the reasons she needed to avoid this man.

She settled into a corner of the swing. This was the time of day Jenn liked best. The sun had set and the sky was a deep blue fading into the purple of twilight.

She leaned her head back and closed her eyes. She could hear the clatter of dishes from inside the house and the sound of muted conversation.

After only a little while, the noise stopped and the screen door opened. "I sent Zack upstairs to take a shower. Can he do that by himself?"

"He can handle it." She laughed. "He looked like he rolled around in the dirt."

Jenn felt the fine tension Trace's presence always caused in her. It was if he brought some kind of electrical charge with him. She pushed against the floorboards of the porch with her toe to get the swing going, as if the motion could distract her from the draw of this man.

Trace stayed by the door, and Jenn realized he was waiting for an invitation to join her.

"Why don't you sit down for a while before you go?" She wanted to ask him about the Stone family, since it looked as if Kelly was already on her way to being totally gone on Ryan. Right, she told herself. That's the only reason she'd offered half her swing.

Trace settled into the rocking chair on the other side of the porch. Jenn relaxed a little at the distance he had placed between them. Before she could ask her question, Trace asked one of his own.

"Jenn, I know you're on vacation, but I really need your help."

Vacation? she thought. Vacations were when you stayed in a hotel with room service and went out to dinner every night. This was no vacation. But she kept that thought to herself and gave him a noncommittal "What's up?"

"The land swindle."

"Oh." She'd already told him no.

"I'm trying to investigate, but I'm stuck. I really need someone with your skills."

Warning bells went off in Jenn's head. There was no way she could afford to spend more time with Trace. He was already taking up too much space in her thoughts.

"Can't you get someone from the county? They must have people who do the same thing I do."

Trace shrugged in the gathering darkness. "I've made requests twice. Budget cuts."

She understood. Her department had taken several cuts, too. "I don't think I'll be here long enough to help out." Her excuse sounded lame and weak, but she had to protect herself. The draw to Trace was too strong.

The silence stretched out between them.

"Technically I shouldn't tell you this," he finally said. "Miranda's husband lost a bundle. He came to see me before he left town."

Jenn was shocked. Miranda hadn't said a word about Roger losing money, and her sister had certainly not been shy about listing her soon-to-be ex-husband's faults and misdeeds.

"She didn't mention it." Then a thought occurred to her. "I don't think she knows." Roger had handled all the money. When Miranda had tried to access their joint account after he ran off, she found it had been closed. Miranda assumed he'd taken all the money, but maybe it had been gone before he left.

"That would explain some of his behavior," Jenn murmured.

"If we recover any of the money people lost, Miranda would stand to get a share."

Her sister could definitely use the cash. "Let me think about it."

"I would appreciate any help you could give me. Just some basic information on how to track this would help."

"I'll think about it," she repeated. She was torn. On one hand, it would be a way to help her sister. Miranda had stubbornly refused money when Jenn had offered. On the other hand, she would have to spend time with Trace, and she wasn't sure she trusted her resolve to resist him.

They sat in silence until the phone rang. Kelly's voice drifted out of the upstairs window. Jenn could tell by her tone she was talking to a boy. She guessed it was Ryan Stone.

"What do you know about the Stone family?"

It had gotten so dark she could just see his silhouette on the other side of the porch.

"Just what I heard at the Bee Hive. Stone moved his family here from Houston. Made money in the oil business and decided to try the country life. Why?"

Because, Jenn wanted to say, Kelly looks at him

the way I used to look at you. Instead she said, "He was talking to Kelly today in the barn. I wondered if he was the one who gave her a ride to the party, but he said they moved here Saturday."

"I knew all the kids at the party. I haven't met him yet."

Their short companionable silence ended when a car turned into the driveway.

"I think you're about to meet the Stone boy."

Jenn's instincts had been right. Ryan emerged from the car and walked onto the porch. "Good evening, Miss Williams. Is Kelly home?"

Jenn hid a smile at his question. She was sure he'd been on the phone with Kelly not five minutes ago and knew full well her niece was home.

Jenn made a quick decision. Kelly was not supposed to leave the house without Jenn, but Jenn wouldn't turn the boy away the first time he called on her niece.

Jenn gestured toward Trace. "Ryan, this is Sheriff McCabe."

Ryan crossed the porch and shook hands with Trace. "Nice to meet you, sir."

Jenn stood and said, "Let me go see if she's available."

She found Kelly sitting at the top of the stairs.

She walked up and sat down on the step beside her niece. "Ryan's here."

Kelly flushed and nodded. "I know.'

"Then why are you still up here?"

"Aunt Jenn, I didn't want him to think I was too available!" she said in a fierce whisper.

Jenn smiled. "You're right. Keep him guessing, Kel."

Kelly rubbed at a nonexistent spot on her knee, giving her jeans her full attention. "Aunt Jenn, what if he wants me to go out with him?"

Jenn raised an eyebrow. "Tonight?"

Kelly nodded.

"Say no."

Kelly thought about that for a minute. "Because I don't want him to think I'm too easy?"

Jenn patted Kelly on the knee. "No, because you're still grounded."

Kelly groaned. "That is so, like, unfair."

Jenn shook her head at her niece's halfhearted argument. "No. That is so, like, my decision. But I'll talk to your mom tomorrow and maybe we'll spring you next week."

Kelly smiled, then turned serious again. "Okay. Can he stay here and watch TV?"

Jenn nodded. "For an hour. Downstairs in the living room."

Kelly rolled her eyes, but seemed to know better than to argue. "Okay."

"You don't have to tell him you're grounded. Just offer the invite." Jenn had no doubt the boy would do whatever Kelly suggested.

As Kelly started down the steps, Jenn went to check on her son and found him sprawled facedown

on his bed, his hair still wet from the shower, sound
asleep. She leaned over and kissed him good-night,
then closed the door.

Not quite ready to return to the porch, where Trace
waited, she sat back down on the top step. Could she
help Trace and not give in to her feelings from the
past? Could she refuse now that she knew Miranda
was involved?

By the time she got downstairs, Kelly and Ryan
were sitting at either end of the couch watching TV.
Trace still sat in the rocker at the far end of the porch.

Jenn settled in the chair beside him so they could
talk without Kelly overhearing. "Zack is out cold."

Trace chuckled. "Big day."

"Thanks. It meant a lot to him."

Trace nodded, then jerked his head toward the
sound of the TV coming out the screen door. In a low
voice he said, "Something about Ryan worry you?"

"He seems like a nice enough kid." But, she
thought again, Kelly looks at him the same way I
used to look at you. And she knew how much hurt
that could lead to.

"But?" Trace prompted.

Jenn improvised. "She's young. And it's been a
rough time for her. I'd like to know he hasn't been
in trouble." It wouldn't be the first time a family had
moved their teenager to the country hoping for a
fresh start.

Trace nodded. "I'll nose around and see what I can
find out. Unofficially."

Jenn felt a little guilty about checking up on the boy when she had no reason to doubt he was anything but what he seemed. But she wanted Trace to protect Kelly. "I'd appreciate that."

"No problem," he said quietly.

He had relaxed into the chair. His head was back and his eyes closed.

"Trace?"

"Yeah?" he said, turning his head without lifting it off the back of the chair, and looking at her. His body was completely at ease, but his eyes were warm and alert.

She swallowed hard, thinking she was probably making a big mistake. "I'll take a look at your investigation. With one condition."

"Thanks. I need the help."

She waited for him to ask, and when he didn't she said, "Don't you want to know what the condition is?"

She saw him grin, his teeth showing whitely in the dark. He leaned over and slid his hand around her arm. The warmth of his palm and the friction of his skin on hers sent a shiver through her that had her breasts tingling and her toes curling.

He pulled her close and whispered in her ear. "What's the condition, Jenn?" His tongue traced the rim of her ear.

"I, uh…" All rational thought left her as his lips traveled south. He kissed the side of her neck, working his way down to her collarbone.

When her breathing became labored and her

bones started to feel as if they were melting, he stood up and said, "Thanks for supper, Jenn. I'll see you tomorrow."

He was leaving? Just like that? She couldn't even remember what she'd been about to say. She watched him saunter toward his car and felt as if she'd been had, in more ways than one.

Chapter Twelve

The next day Jenn glanced in the rearview mirror at Zack, then fumbled with her cell phone, keeping one eye on the road. Fortunately traffic was nonexistent. She'd never attempt to answer her phone while driving in Dallas.

"Hello?"

"Ms. Williams?"

Jenn recognized the clipped voice of the head nurse on the morning shift at the hospital. She'd spoken to her just over an hour ago. Jenn called every morning after shift change to check on Miranda.

The no-nonsense tone of the woman's voice had her heart racing. Jenn pulled over to the side of the road. "Yes?"

"I wanted to let you know Miranda is going into the delivery room."

Jenn's heart missed a few beats. "What happened?"

"Why don't you come on over and I'll fill you in when you get here?"

Jenn wasn't going to waste time arguing with her. "Okay. I'll be there as quickly as I can." She disconnected the call.

Zack signed that he wanted to know what was going on. He might be deaf, but he had an uncanny ability to read body language and facial expressions, even in a rearview mirror.

Jenn signaled him to wait, then pulled back onto the road. She parked in front of C.J.'s house and quickly explained the situation to her son. By the time she finished, Zack's playmate and his mother had come out to greet them.

"Denise, I need a big favor. I just got a call from the hospital and Miranda's having her baby."

Denise waved her hand in a dismissive gesture. "I'll keep Zack. Let him spend the night. He can wear a pair of C.J.'s pajamas and I'll find a toothbrush for him."

Relieved, Jenn said, "Thanks. I owe you. Call me if there's a problem." She told Zack he was spending the night, and both the boys whooped and galloped into the house.

Stomach churning, Jenn got back in her car to go back to the fairgrounds to get Kelly. She pulled up at the back gate and explained to the security guard that she had an emergency. He let her drive through.

She jumped out of her car and ran into the barn. Kelly was standing by Petunia's pen, talking to Ryan Stone. Both of them seemed oblivious to the din of Petunia and her litter as they crowded the enclosure next to the teenagers.

Kelly spotted Jenn and blinked in surprise. "Aunt Jenn, what—"

Jenn made an impatient gesture toward the door. "Come on, Kelly, we have to go. Your mom's having the baby."

Kelly's eyes got big and she swallowed. She blushed furiously and turned away from Ryan. "Just a minute," she mumbled. "I haven't fed the pigs yet."

Ryan took Kelly's hand. "Ms. Williams, I can bring Kelly as soon as we're done here."

Jenn didn't miss the grateful look her niece sent the boy. If she hadn't fallen for him before this, the girl was a goner now.

Jenn considered the plan, then decided it might be better if she spoke to the staff at the hospital before Kelly got there. "Okay." She pointed a finger at Ryan. "But drive safely. And use your seat belts."

Ryan nodded solemnly.

Kelly rolled her eyes and hefted a bag of feed. "This will just take a few minutes."

Nerves strung tight as wire, Jenn raced back to her car and didn't follow her own advice. She broke the speed limit on the way to the hospital.

She ran through the lobby, and dodged huge metal carts delivering breakfast to the patients. The familiar smells of the hospital only added to her anxiety as she took the stairs to the second floor, unwilling to wait for the elevator.

When she got to the empty nurses' station she spotted the head nurse coming out of a patient's room across the hallway.

"Miranda?" she asked, breathless from her dash into the building as well as the anxiety that had been building since she'd received the phone call.

The nurse smiled reassuringly. "No word yet."

She took Jenn by the arm and walked her back to the nurses' station. She picked up a green plastic strip and deftly placed it around Jenn's wrist, then handed Jenn another strip with Kelly's name on it.

"Why don't you go down to the waiting room and I'll send the doctor as soon as he comes out."

"What happened?" She couldn't just wait. She needed information.

"Miranda started having contractions again and the resident did a stress test on the baby early this morning. Her doctor came in and decided this was a good time to deliver," she said in a soothing tone.

Stress test? Did that mean something was wrong with the baby? Why hadn't Miranda called her? There was something the nurse wasn't telling her. "Is there a problem?" she demanded.

The nurse reached out and patted Jenn reassuringly on the arm. "It should go fine."

How could she be sure? Frustrated and scared, Jenn nodded tightly and waited for Kelly by the elevators, too nervous to sit. After what seemed like an eternity the bell indicating the arrival of the elevator sounded and Kelly came hurtling through the open door.

"Where's Mom?"

Jenn pasted on a smile. No need to get Kelly upset. "She's in the delivery room."

Kelly eyed her suspiciously. "What's wrong?"

Obviously she hadn't fooled her niece for a second. It was time to be honest. "Probably nothing. I'm just scared."

"Me, too," Kelly said in a small voice.

"Let's go sit over there where we can see the doctor coming out of the delivery room."

"Okay." She let Jenn lead her to a row of ugly orange plastic chairs opposite the nurses' station.

"Where's Ryan?"

Kelly shrugged. "He went back to clean out the pigpen, then he has a dentist appointment."

Jenn studied her niece as she fastened the ID bracelet around the girl's slender wrist. Trying to break the tension, she said, "Ah, a man who'll shovel pig poop for you. He's a keeper."

Kelly didn't answer, but her face turned pink.

"You didn't want him here, did you?"

"Oh, Aunt Jenn. It's so totally mortifying," she wailed.

"What is?"

"Mom having a baby. All my friends knowing that she was, well, you know."

Jenn coughed to cover her smile. "Yes, I know."

The thought that a parent might be having sex was too much for teenagers to handle. "Did you tell him your mom was going to have a baby?"

"I was going to. Soon," she added sheepishly. "He said he thought it was cool." She didn't look as if she had believed him.

Before Jenn could reply, the doors to the delivery room. Miranda's doctor pulled off his mask and cap. He looked tired and distracted.

"Miranda?" Jenn asked, her stomach squeezed in knots.

He gave her a weary smile. "Is fine. And so is the baby."

Jenn gulped back a sob of relief. "Can we see her?"

He nodded. "Delivery room two."

"Thank you!" Jenn and Kelly pushed through the double doors. They came to a halt outside the open door and peeked inside. Miranda, looking drawn and exhausted, lay propped up in the bed.

She spotted them and managed a tired smile. "Hey, you two."

Jenn and Kelly came to the side of the bed.

"Hi, Mom," Kelly said, and bent to kiss Miranda on the cheek. Miranda's hand, IV tubes still attached, came around her daughter's slender back.

Kelly stepped back and Jenn leaned down to kiss her sister. "How are you feeling?"

Miranda gave a tired huff of laughter. "Like a wet rag. Did you see him?" Her face shone with an expression of peace.

"Not yet." Jenn looked around. The room was empty. No incubator. "So it's a boy?"

Miranda nodded. "He's little, but he's healthy."

Kelly looked over at Jenn and raised her eyebrows.

Miranda looked back and forth between them and said, "What was that look for? Did you two have a bet?"

Kelly giggled. "No. When we went to the for-tune-teller at the fair she mentioned the baby. She said 'him' when she talked about him."

Miranda shrugged and smiled. "Well, she had a fifty-fifty chance of being right."

Jenn nodded, then added, "She also said Kelly would fall in love."

Kelly blushed furiously.

Miranda eyed her sister and her daughter. "Why do I get the feeling you're not telling me something? Or is this about the new boy?"

"Mom!" Kelly wailed, sounding utterly mortified.

Jenn and Miranda laughed.

"Nice to see everyone in such good spirits," one of the nurses said, "but I need you to leave so we can get Mom here cleaned up and back in her room."

Miranda caught Kelly's hand. "Why don't you go and introduce yourself to your baby brother?"

"Good idea," Jenn said. "We'll be back after you've had a chance to rest."

At the nursery, the nurse behind the desk was dressed in cheerful turquoise scrubs covered with tiny teddy bears. She asked for their names, the baby's name and their relation to him. Then she checked their ID bracelets and told them to have a seat.

She disappeared into a glassed-in room and returned with a tiny blue bundle in her arms.

"Who's first?" she asked.

Suddenly feeling shaky, Jenn pointed at Kelly. "I think the big sister should have the honors," she said, not able to take her eyes off the tiny blanket-wrapped bundle.

The nurse lowered the baby into Kelly's waiting arms, and Kelly uttered a small cry of delight. "Oh, look at him. He's so tiny and perfect!" She held him with one arm and folded the blanket back from his tiny red face. "What's your name, little guy?"

Jenn felt her chest tighten as Kelly cooed over her baby brother, wondering if the fortune-teller had been right all along.

Was this the second time this summer Kelly would fall in love? Jenn suspected it was. All the animosity the teenager had harbored over her mother's pregnancy had disappeared.

Kelly turned in her chair. "Your turn, Auntie Jenn." Gently she held the baby toward Jenn.

Jenn felt frozen in her chair.

"Aunt Jenn?"

Jenn forced herself to reach for the child, and as soon as her nephew's warm weight settled in her arms she felt the breath back up in her lungs. Her heart pounded and tiny beads of perspiration broke out on her brow. Panicked by the unexpected physical reaction, she held the baby as if he were an explosive device that could blow up at any moment.

"Aunt Jenn, are you okay?" Kelly asked, her voice full of concern.

"Yes. No. I don't know." Her eyes burned and her vision blurred. She realized she was holding her breath, but she couldn't seem to draw in any air. Tears flooded her eyes and dripped unchecked down her cheeks.

The nurse appeared in her line of sight, and took the baby out of Jenn's stiff arms. "Let's get him back on the warming table," she said in a soothing voice.

Jenn, mortified by her reaction, couldn't seem to get hold of herself. She could feel Kelly rubbing her arm and knew the girl must be scared, but Jenn had lost her self-control.

The nurse returned and knelt in front of Jenn. "Are you okay?"

Jenn's vision blurred again as she tried to catch her breath. Her inhalations turned into gulping sobs. She shook her head.

"The quiet room the lactation nurse uses is empty right now. Let's get you in there so you can rest."

Jenn let Kelly and the nurse lead her into the room and put her on the couch.

Trace was thinking of Jenn as he stacked the last of the fraud-investigation files on his desk.

Henrie buzzed him. "Sheriff, Kelly Roberts is on line three."

"Thanks, Henrie." Trace punched a button on the phone. "Hey, Kelly," he said, wondering what the teenager wanted.

"Sheriff, can you come to the hospital? It's Aunt Jenn." The girl's voice trembled.

Cold fear gripped his heart. Something had happened to Jenn. Trace stood up so quickly his chair slammed back against the wall. "What happened? Is Jenn okay?"

Kelly took a deep breath. "I don't think so. Mom had her baby and we were holding him and Aunt Jenn got really upset. I don't know why. Mom's asleep and I didn't think I should wake her. I didn't know who else to call."

Trace made a conscious effort to slow his breathing as his relief sank in. Jenn wasn't physically hurt. "You did good, honey. Just stay with your aunt and I'll be there in a few minutes."

"Okay. Hurry. We're on the second floor, near the nursery," she said, clearly scared.

Trace hung up and ran to his cruiser. He made it to the second floor of the hospital in record time. Kelly stood in an open doorway, clutching a box of tissues. Muted sounds of sobbing came from the room.

The girl, her face pale, gestured to the room as she whispered, "I didn't know what to do. She can't stop crying."

Trace put his hand on her shoulder and drew her out into the hallway. He had no idea if the girl knew about the baby he and Jenn had lost.

"I'm glad you called me. Why don't you go sit with your mom for a while? Don't upset her with this just now. I'll come down and talk to her after I take care of Jenn."

Kelly hesitated and glanced into the darkened room behind her, then nodded, shoved the box of tissues into his hand and took off toward the maternity patients' rooms.

Jenn lying on a couch facing the back wall, curled up like a child. She trembled and shook as she cried.

He sat down on the edge of the couch, dropped the tissues on the floor and rubbed Jenn's back. She felt fragile under his hand.

"Go away, please." Her voice was a watery, gulping whisper.

He kept rubbing. "Not a chance of that, sweetheart," he said, relieved that she seemed to be calming down.

Trace scooped Jenn into his arms and cradled her on his lap. She nestled into his chest and took in a shuddering sigh.

It didn't take a genius to figure out why she was so upset. "Can you tell me what happened?" He pushed several tissues into her hand. Jenn needed to talk, and this time he wasn't letting go of her until she did.

She took a swipe at her eyes, then blew her nose. "I don't know." She tried to laugh, but it sounded more like a little sob.

"Why don't you tell me about this morning?"

She was quiet for a long time, then she nestled in closer. "The hospital called while I was on the way to drop Zack off. They said Miranda was going into the delivery room."

She related the story of coming to the hospital, and seeing Miranda after the baby was born. Then she became very still and quiet.

"Kelly told me you got to see the baby," he prompted.

Jenn nodded, her cheek rubbing against his shirt.

"Jenn, is the baby okay?"

She nodded again. "He's little, but they said he's fine."

"What happened when you held the baby, Jenn?" He was no psychologist, but he was pretty sure he knew.

"I don't know exactly. I just started to shake and I couldn't catch my breath. I know he's okay, but I was so scared for him. I'm sure I scared Kelly. I know I scared myself."

She tried to sit up, but he held her where she was. "Just stay here for a minute. I need to ask you a question."

She relaxed back against him and said, "Okay" in a weary, resigned voice.

It took him a moment to ask the difficult question. He knew he was treading on very emotional territory, but Jenn needed to face what had happened.

"Were you thinking of Miranda's baby while you were holding him, or were you thinking of the baby you lost? Our baby?"

Jenn stiffened and went very still. Just when Trace was sure she wasn't going to answer, she said in a whisper, "I'm not sure."

He could see her struggling for control as he smoothed the hair back from her face. "Did you cry when you lost the baby?"

He wanted her to let go, to feel what she hadn't allowed herself to feel all those years ago.

She was quiet for a long moment, then she cleared her throat. "No. Mama wouldn't let me."

He waited through another long silence, trying his best not to damn her mother, and failing. He knew Jenn. She needed time now to put it all together.

"She even made me sleep with her that night. She said it would be wicked to cry." Her voice hitched on another sob.

Finally she let out a sigh and shuddered. "I didn't even remember that until just now."

"Eight years is a long time to hold grief in, Jenn. You needed to let it go. Feel better?"

She nodded. For the first time since he'd arrived, she looked up at him, her face blotchy and her eyes swollen.

Trace thought she looked incredibly beautiful.

"Did you cry?" she asked in a small, hesitant voice.

"Yes." His own eyes filled with tears, and he gathered her even closer, holding her until she finally slept.

Chapter Thirteen

Jenn sat in the conference room adjoining Trace's office and opened the last case file on the land fraud deal that had suckered so many of the residents of Blossom County, including her sister's soon-to-be ex-husband.

She'd been working for days. She could see a definite trail, but so far she'd been unable to trace the dealings back to any source. On top of that, there were probably victims they didn't know about. She suspected many people hadn't reported their loss because of embarrassment.

Perhaps it was time to run the story in the newspaper, let the citizens know how many people had been swindled. Perhaps that would flush out more leads. The only thing she was certain of right now was that at least one of the criminals had to have access to bank records.

She made a note to Trace to check with the banks in town. Maybe they'd had trouble with hackers just before the swindle, or maybe they'd fired some employees.

Jenn closed the last file and rolled her shoulders. It was just about time to pick up Zack, then head to the fair and check in on Kelly. She had a lot to do, because tonight she would be bringing Miranda and the baby home from the hospital.

She sighed and stared at the even, tidy stacks of folders, thinking of what had happened the day her nephew had been born. There was no other word for it. She'd had a breakdown.

She traced her finger over the writing on the outside of the top folder. That rather dramatic release of emotions had left her wrung out but more at peace than she had been in a long time.

She had Trace to thank for that.

He'd been there for her. Big, solid and warm, he'd held her and comforted her until she remembered everything she'd tried to bury for eight years.

She had to admit that her feelings for him were as strong as they had been eight years ago.

She carefully lined up her pencils and pens as she wondered. *Why* she had been so set on keeping her distance from him?

But she knew the answer. She had been trying to protect herself. Not from him, but from her own feelings. Was that why she had dragged her feet about finalizing the annulment?

She looked at her perfectly aligned row of pens and pencils and shook her head. They were arranged by size and color. Control. Trace was right. She *did* always want control. That was the only way she felt comfortable.

She used a fingertip to knock the middle pen out of alignment. What would happen if she let go a little? What would happen if she stopped fighting her feelings and gave in to them? How would she feel in a month if she went back to Dallas and had never explored what was between them? She remembered an old saying that claimed you didn't regret the things you'd done, but rather the things you *hadn't* done.

Did she want to spend the rest of her life wondering?

They were both adults. Heck, they were still married.

She propped her elbows on the table and rested her chin on her folded hands. What would be so bad about exploring some possibilities before she went back to Dallas?

She was pretty sure Trace would be willing.

The more she thought about it, the more she liked the idea. So did certain parts of her body, which had started to warm up and tingle.

As teenagers they'd made hurried love in the backseat of his car, fearful of discovery. What would it be like to have a leisurely night with him as adults?

"What are you thinking about?"

Her head jerked up at the sound of his voice and she felt a blush creep up her cheeks.

He was standing in the doorway between his office and the conference room. He'd changed out of his uniform and was wearing jeans and a blue cotton shirt.

He looked good in blue, she thought, warming even more under his gaze.

"You." Jenn smiled and wondered what he would do if he knew what she was thinking. "Did I thank you for being such a good friend?"

She saw a tight look cross his face. It lasted only a second, then his expression relaxed into a smile. "Yeah. You told me." He stepped into the room. "Time for a break."

Jenn stood and stretched. She didn't miss the way his eyes followed her movements.

She shook her head and glanced at her watch. "Time to go get Zack."

"Okay. I'll treat you both to lunch."

Jenn tried not to think about what she'd really like to do over the lunch hour. After all, she had responsibilities. Lots of them. "I have to go to the fairgrounds and check on Kelly."

Now that the possibility of making love to him had occurred to her, she couldn't seem to think of anything else.

He smiled. "So we'll have lunch at the fair. After lunch I'll buy you a deep-fried Twinkie."

Jenn groaned, her stomach rebelling. "I'll go if we skip the Twinkie."

He laughed and turned back into his office. "Sure. Whatever you want," he said over his shoulder.

She gave him a long look. He still had a great rear end, especially in jeans. She knew what she wanted. And it had nothing to do with food.

She wanted him.

They walked out together into the bright hot day. The sun felt good on her bare arms. Trace kept his office as cold as a meat locker, which really didn't surprise her. He threw off a lot of body heat. She'd noticed that while sitting on his lap at the hospital.

What would the past eight years have been like if that had happened right after she'd lost the baby? If she hadn't run away from the tragedy? From him?

"Jenn?" He put his hand on her arm.

She jerked to a stop, all her attention on his warm palm. "Yes?" She really needed to stop daydreaming.

He studied her face. "What's on your mind?"

She shrugged and tried to act casual. "Lots. Miranda and the baby are coming home tonight."

Trace let go of her arm and raised an eyebrow, looking unconvinced. "Does he have a name yet?"

She never had been any good at hiding her thoughts from him. "Not yet. Miranda's still thinking about it."

"Does Roger know the baby's been born?"

Jenn shook her head. "He's someplace in Mexico. Apparently he made it pretty clear before he left that he had no interest."

Trace's expression tightened. "I don't give a damn about his interest. He has a responsibility."

Jenn nodded. Some men were good with responsibility. Some weren't. Miranda's husband fell into the second category.

She started walking toward her car. "Right now I need to pick up my little responsibility."

He grabbed her hand and pulled her in the other direction. "Let's take my truck. There's something I need to drop off on the way."

She followed him toward his truck and saw a large plaster turtle in the bed. "What's this?"

"Another kidnapping. This one came with a note that said, and I quote, 'I'm not going to race the rabbit anymore.'"

Jenn laughed and shook her head. "Well, whoever is doing this certainly has a sense of humor."

She had to hitch her skirt up a bit to step on the high running board. Trace's intake of breath made her feel feminine and desirable. She settled in with a smile.

Oh, yes, she was definitely going to think about spending some time alone with Trace.

Even with the windows down, the inside of the truck was stuffy and the upholstery was hot on the backs of her legs. Nothing like Texas in the summer.

Trace walked around to the driver's door and swung up into the seat. "It'll all stop as soon as school starts. Unfortunately the kids are targeting the people in town who think the younger generation is going to, and again I quote, 'heck in a hand basket.'"

"I remember them saying something similar about us."

He grinned. "Yeah. Jason and I were talking about that just the other day."

Jenn laughed and glanced over at his handsome profile as he turned the key in the ignition. "If people knew what kind of trouble their mayor and sheriff caused fifteen years ago, you guys would be out of office in a heartbeat."

Trace put the truck in reverse. "You thinking about blackmail?"

She smiled at him. "Only if you make me eat a deep-fried Twinkie."

They both laughed. Jenn felt so good that she and Trace were finally friends again. She realized she'd missed that almost as much as his love.

Jenn stood beside Trace and Zack, eyeing the Tilt-a-Whirl as it spun around, the people on it screaming and yelling.

"Zack, sweetie, I really don't like rides like this." Especially after just eating a hot dog and an ice cream cone.

Trace winked at Jenn and grabbed the boy's hand. He pulled him into line as the ride came to a halt. "Come on. We'll let the sissies sit this one out," he said, his comment directed at Jenn.

Zack turned and waved at her, a look of pure delight on his face.

She fought the urge to grab him back. The midway rides scared her, but she let him go. She always encouraged Zack to embrace life despite his handicap, and reluctantly she supposed this was part of it.

Trace and Zack climbed into their seats and fastened their harnesses. Trace leaned over and double-checked Zack's buckle. The ride started, and as they flashed by, Trace and Zack had identical expressions on their faces. Delighted terror. What was it about the male of the species that craved speed and danger?

When the ride slowed, she sighed in relief.

Zack grabbed Trace's hand as they walked toward her. "Can I talk you into the Ferris wheel?" Trace asked.

Jenn nodded. "Now, that's a ride I like!"

Trace leaned down, pointed to the huge revolving wheel, then awkwardly signed, "Want to?"

Zack nodded and took off in the direction of the wheel.

Trace caught her hand and held it. "He's a great kid, Jenn. You've done quite a job."

"Thanks." She didn't feel she could take credit for Zack. He'd been very special when she'd met him. But Trace's praise made her feel good. So did his big warm hand, wrapped around hers.

They eased into the line for the Ferris wheel with Zack. When it was their turn, Trace guided Zack in first. It was a tight fit on the seat, and Jenn was flush with Trace's warm body. To make more room, he put his arm around her, drawing her close to his side.

She had a sudden memory of the last time she'd been on a Ferris wheel. It had been eight years ago, with Trace, right here at the fairgrounds. The summer she'd gotten pregnant. Longing for him left her breathless. She shifted and settled in for the ride.

"Comfortable?" he asked in a low tone.

She shivered in anticipation and gave him a slow smile. "Oh, yes."

He nodded, never taking his eyes off her as his hand caressed her bare arm. His expression told her he knew what she was thinking. She blushed.

As they got to the top of the wheel, he kissed her, a long, slow, deep kiss that had her toes curling in her sandals.

"Tradition," he whispered in her ear, sending shivers down her spine.

He'd always kissed her at the top of the ride.

As the wheel brought them down she kissed him back. Another tradition.

A small hand pulled at her skirt to get her attention. Good heavens. She'd almost forgotten Zack was along on the ride. She leaned forward, and Zack pointed to a line of angry-looking black clouds in the distance.

"That looks like quite a front," Trace said as his cell phone rang.

He leaned on one hip and unclipped his phone from his belt. "McCabe. Yeah. I'm on the Ferris wheel now looking at it. Check with the weather service again in ten minutes and call me back."

As their basket reached the bottom of the ride, he nodded at the clouds. "This line of storms should

miss us, but there's a lot more weather coming in behind this. I need to get going."

"Do you have time to give us a ride back to my
car?" She was still parked behind the courthouse.
"Zack is spending the night with his friend C.J. and
I need to drop him off before I get Miranda."

"Sure. Let's stop and get Kelly."

The temperature dropped noticeably and the wind
kicked up as they hurried to the barns.

But Kelly wasn't there. Just when Jenn thought she
and her niece had gotten back on solid ground with the
trust issues, she was not where she was supposed to be.

Trace untied a string holding a piece of paper
around the top bar of the pig's enclosure. He glanced
at the note, then passed it over to Jenn.

Apparently Ryan had taken Kelly to the feed store
in town to get some eye ointment for the piglets,
then he was going to drop her off at the house.

Jenn eased back on her temper. At least Kelly had
left a note and was on an errand for her 4H project.
She shot a glance at Trace, who was leaning over the
pen looking at the baby pigs.

If that was really where her niece had gone.

At Kelly's age Jenn had made up stories for her
mother and then she'd gone out to Denton Pond to
spend the afternoon swimming and necking with
Trace. She'd needed him as much as she'd needed air
to breathe.

She wished she could spend this afternoon with
him at the pond.

Just the two of them.

She sighed in frustration as she watched him sign to Zack. Between her sister, the new baby, her niece and Zack, where was she going to find time to get him alone?

Trace looked up and gave her a slow smile. She returned the smile, and from the look on his face, it seemed he understood exactly what she was thinking.

Chapter Fourteen

By the time Jenn got home, the entire sky had turned a bruised shade of purple.

There was a message from Miranda on the machine. "Hey," Jenn greeted her sister. "All packed up and ready to come home?"

"Actually, I'm going to stay until tomorrow." She sounded dejected and tired.

Immediately concerned, Jenn asked, "What's the matter?"

"Nothing, really. I'm running a little temperature, and I'm getting some antibiotics, so they won't let me go."

Immediately Jenn wanted to talk to the doctor. "I'll come on over."

"Really, Jenn, I'd rather you didn't. I'm tired,

and I'm going to take a nap. Besides, I can see the storm coming from my window. You stay home with the kids."

"Are you sure it's nothing serious?"

"Positive. Stop being such a worrywart. My doctor assured me it happens all the time."

"Okay," she said, still not fully convinced. "Get some rest and I'll call you in the morning."

Lightning lit the sky and a crack of thunder split the silence. Kelly hadn't arrived yet, and now Jenn wished she had returned Kelly's cell phone. At least she'd be able to track the girl down.

Jenn made a quick call to C.J.'s house and was assured the boys were going to spend the evening in the basement watching videos and playing games. She decided to try the Stone family. If Ryan had a cell phone she could get Kelly that way. She called information and was told the Stones had no listing.

The thought that Kelly and Ryan might be out, oblivious to the tornado watches, frightened Jenn.

Frustrated, she decided to call Trace. He might be able to get her the Stones' number. She picked up the phone, and the lights in the kitchen flickered and the phone line went dead. Her cell phone had a circuits-busy signal.

Jenn grabbed her keys. Better to drive to his office right now, before the weather got worse. She knew he'd be able to help her find Kelly.

She left a note on the kitchen table in case Kelly came home before Jenn could track her down, and headed out to her car. The temperature had dropped another twenty degrees and she pulled on a sweater.

By the time she got out of her car at the court-house, the wind yanked at her skirt and rain pelted her head and shoulders. She pulled her sweater over her head and ran for the sheriff's office. She pushed open the door to find Trace sitting at Henrie's desk.

"What the heck are you doing here?" he said, his voice short and curt.

He certainly didn't sound pleased to see her, but his tone didn't do anything to stop the warm feelings that seeing him caused low in her belly. "I can't find Kelly. I need your help."

"Geez, Jenn, you should have called. You shouldn't be out driving in this storm." He gestured toward the rain-lashed windows.

"I know that! The power is out and the phone is dead at Miranda's, and all I could get on my cell was a circuits-busy signal."

His expression softened as she said, "I tried infor-mation, and they have no listing for the Stone fam-ily. If I can get in touch with them, they might know where Kelly is."

He grabbed her hand as he scooped his cell phone off the desk. "Let me call my contact at the phone company." His big hand wrapped around hers, his touch reassuring her.

She let him lead her back to his office, relieved that she'd come to him.

Trace dialed a number and had a short conversation, then let go of her as he jotted a number on a piece of paper. "Here it is."

As she dialed the number he stood beside her with his hand on her shoulder. A woman answered. "This is Jenn Williams. I'm looking for my niece, Kelly. I think she's with your son Ryan."

"She's here. She tried to call you, but couldn't get an answer. I told her she couldn't leave. I didn't want Ryan driving in this storm."

Jenn sighed with relief and Trace gave her shoulder a squeeze before letting her go. "I just wanted to know she's safe."

"She's fine." Ryan's mother's voice was full of reassurance. "I sent them out to bring in the patio furniture. Do you want to talk with her?"

"No. Could you keep her there until the storm has passed, then I'll come and get her?"

"Of course."

"Thanks." She hung up.

Trace was sitting on the edge of his desk, quietly watching her. "What's up, Jenn?"

Before she could think of an answer the radio crackled with sound. The chief of police in the little town west of them was reporting a funnel cloud had been sighted.

Jenn's heart jumped into her throat.

Trace caught her hand and pulled her toward him, until she stood between his legs. He ran a palm up and down her arm. "Hey, you heard what he said.

"It's heading east. Kelly and Zack and the hospital are all south of here."

He put out a general call to all his deputies as well as fire personnel, rescue workers and the hospital's emergency room to advise them of the situation. Then he activated the emergency sirens.

Her thoughts were much louder than the scream of the warning sirens. Tornadoes didn't stay on any set course. They could change direction any second.

"Come on," he said. "We'll go down to the emergency shelter in the basement, just in case it clips us."

She followed him to the stairs, and halfway down the lights went out. The emergency lights flickered on, bathing the stairwell and empty cells in a murky yellow glow.

"I've never been down here."

Trace laughed. "I didn't think you had. We reserve this area for the people we arrest."

He led her into a reinforced cinder-blocked room designated as the emergency shelter. There were four desks with phones and radios at one end, and boxes of supplies stacked floor to ceiling at the other. Along one wall sat an old brown leather couch.

"Wasn't that your couch?" Her face heated. If she was right, it was out of Trace's parents' den. She and Trace had spent some interesting times on that couch when his folks had been away from home.

He put his arm around her. "Yup. When Mom moved to Florida, she was going to sell it at a yard sale. I told her it had too many good memories for me. So I kept it."

What he was implying sank in and Jenn nearly choked. "You didn't say that to your mother!"

He wrapped his arms around her and smiled down into her face. "Sure I did. She thought I meant all the time I spent on it watching cartoons on Saturday mornings."

Jenn laughed and leaned her head against his shoulder. She supposed Trace had had as easy a time fooling his mother as she had had fooling hers.

That thought brought her back to Kelly. She sighed and moved out of his embrace.

He flipped on the radio. "What's going on here, Jenn? What has you so worried?"

How like him to know she needed someone to lean on. "Kelly's falling in love with Ryan."

Trace raised an eyebrow. "And?"

"And she looks at him the way I used to look at you!"

"Is that bad?" he asked, hugging her to his side and planting a tender kiss on her forehead.

"I don't want her to be hurt."

"You're afraid she'll get pregnant." He shifted her so she was facing him, his arms around her shoulders.

She nodded. "The possibility has crossed my mind, yes."

He put one finger under her chin and tipped her head up so he could meet her eyes. "Don't you think this is Miranda's area of responsibility?"

He was probably right, but Miranda hadn't been

the one to see her daughter fall in love. "Miranda has a lot on her plate right now."

"So what are you going to do?"

"I don't know. I wish I did."

Trace backed up, drawing her with him, and propped his hip on the corner of a desk. "Let me ask you something. If Kelly came to you and told you she was pregnant, what would you do?"

Jenn tried to control her fear, but it crowded her, making it hard to think. She tried to back out of his hold, but he wouldn't let her. "I—I don't know."

He watched her, his eyes intense. "Would you turn her away?"

Her gaze shot up to his face. "No!" She could never do that to Kelly.

"Would you demand she get rid of the baby?"

She put her hands up as if to ward off the idea. "Of course not!" Where had these questions come from?

"Would you treat her the way your mother treated you?" he asked, his voice so quiet she had to strain to hear him.

"Never," she whispered.

"No, you wouldn't." He stood up and pulled her into his embrace. "Because your love for her is unconditional. Even if Kelly did the same thing we did, the outcome would be different. Can you see that?"

"Yes." But she still didn't want Kelly to suffer.

His arms tightened around her. "Talk to her. Tell her what happened to us. I think she already suspects a lot."

Jenn let herself settle against his quiet strength. He kissed her gently, his lips a warm whisper against hers. "Jenn, I'm not ashamed of what happened. I'm just sorry it turned out the way it did."

She let that comment sink in. Was she ashamed? Had that colored her thinking all these years and made running away and staying away seem like a good option? She suspected so, but before she could explore that thought in depth, the radio crackled to life.

Several reports came in, one after another, signaling an all clear. The tornado had dissipated, and there was no property damage in the area. Jenn sank into a chair. Thank goodness. Everyone was safe.

"We might as well go back upstairs." Trace took her hand to lead her out of the room.

She followed, thinking about what he'd said. Suddenly he stopped and drew her sideways.

Before she could ask what he was doing, he spun her around and backed her up until her bottom made contact with a wall. He reached to the side, and she heard the sound of metal hitting metal.

She stared up at him. "What are you doing?" She couldn't believe it. He'd closed them in one of the cells.

He kissed her jawline and was working his way across her cheek. "What I wish I'd done eight years ago."

He shifted his weight against her and slid his arm around her waist, pulling her to him and kissing her mouth, using his tongue and teeth on her until she was breathless.

She shoved at his chest and came up for air. What was he thinking? "Trace McCabe, are you crazy?" They were in a jail cell, for pity's sake.

"Yeah, crazy for you." He kissed her again, and this time her legs trembled.

She was crazy for him, too. She put her arms around his neck and hung on. His hands were busy hiking up her skirt.

"What if someone walks in and sees us?" she asked, then lost the thought as her senses reacted to the heat and smell of him.

"We have plenty of time."

She made a strangled sound of need as he caressed the backs of her thighs and worked his way up to her bottom. They should talk, she thought vaguely as the rational part of her brain slid away.

"What are we doing?"

He let out a laugh. "If you have to ask that, I must not be trying hard enough." His hands brushed past her waist and landed warm and heavy on her breasts.

Before she could get a grip on her runaway feelings, she arched into his hands and heard his chest rumble with noise of approval.

"Trace, we shouldn't." Her words sounded half-hearted at best.

"Why not? We're still married. I want you, and I'm pretty sure you want me."

She did. She wanted him with every fiber of her being. She'd relied on Trace so much these past few weeks she *felt* married. Maybe she hadn't filed the annulment because she *wanted* to be married.

Suddenly nothing seemed to matter except his clever warm hands and wicked mouth.

When they were both breathless he broke the kiss and nuzzled her shoulder. He'd lowered the zipper on her dress and pushed the thin straps off her shoulders.

He licked her bare breast and she bit back a groan of pure pleasure.

"I love these little sundresses you wear. I knew you didn't have a bra on." His breath whispered across her wet skin and her knees buckled.

He'd always been able to do that to her.

He turned her around and walked her backward across the dark space until she felt the backs of her knees come up against something hard. He twisted her around and together they dropped onto what must have been the bed.

"Trace," she gasped as he pulled her across his body on the narrow bed, "what if somebody comes?"

He gave a little huff of a laugh and his hand swept up her leg underneath her skirt. "Oh, darlin', I'm counting on it."

He slipped his fingers under the elastic of her panties and found what he was after.

Suddenly she didn't care anymore about anything but him.

He worked his magic on her until she was hot and shaking and crazy for him. Then he settled into her and drove her slowly to distraction.

* * *

Trace pulled Jenn against his side and held her as she slept. He ran his hand over her hair and she snuggled her face into his neck. He sighed and kissed her temple.

He knew now that summer fling was not going to do the job. He wanted the entire package. Marriage, home and family.

He wanted to be a father to her child, and several more babies that he and Jenn would make.

Shaken by the force of his emotion, he realized he was more in love with Jenn than he had ever been in the past.

They belonged together.

Forever.

Chapter Fifteen

A couple of days later, after Miranda and the baby had come home, Jenn went upstairs to check on her sister. And she still couldn't stop thinking about her night with Trace.

She couldn't believe she'd made love with Trace in a jail cell! She grinned. And she'd do it again, given the opportunity.

Not only was she not sorry she'd decided to make love with Trace, she found herself plotting when they could be together again. She wasn't going to be in Blossom for much longer, and she didn't want to miss any opportunities.

At the thought of going back to Dallas and leaving Trace, a shadow fell over the joy she felt.

Don't do it, she told herself. Don't spoil it. She

was going to let go of some of her self-control, just to prove she could. Then she was going back to Dallas and her life.

That was what she wanted. Trace did, too. Otherwise he would have said something. He would have asked her not to go through with the annulment.

She'd see him as much as she could manage while she was here, then she'd return home and take care of the papers.

That was the wise and reasonable thing to do.

She hoped if she kept repeating those words, she could convince herself they were true.

She continued to the top of the stairs and peeked into Miranda's room. Her sister and the baby were both asleep. As quietly as she could, she closed the door. At this point, sleep was more important for Miranda than food. Jenn had heard the baby cry several times during the night and she figured both of them were exhausted.

Jenn had finally gotten up the nerve to hold her nephew. In the past few days she had gotten used to being around him—the baby still didn't have a name. Zack wanted to name him Peter after the main character in the Spider-Man story, but Miranda was not buying that one.

The back door slammed and she hurried down the stairs.

She caught Zack and C.J. in the kitchen. "Where are you going?"

Zack pointed at the ceiling and C.J. said, "Zack's room."

Jenn shook her head. "Baby's sleeping."

The little boys were really wired today. She needed to get them out of the house if Miranda was going to get any rest.

"How about we call C.J.'s mom and see if it's okay to take him to the fair? We can eat lunch there and walk around."

Zack signed, "Go on rides."

Not if she could help it. "We'll see."

Both boys whooped and danced around the kitchen as Jenn called C.J.'s mother and got her permission to take the boy along. Then she called Kelly to tell her they'd be there to bring her lunch. After the storm Jenn had decided to return Kelly's cell phone. At least that way she could reach her niece easily.

Once at the fair the boys insisted on a ride before lunch, and Jenn didn't argue with them. Better to ride on an empty stomach, she reasoned as she stopped at the ticket booth and bought a strip of tickets.

"We went on this one three times in a row on Saturday," C.J. announced, pointing to a ride called the Octopus.

Zack looked suitably impressed, and jumped up and down, jerking on the hem of Jenn's shorts.

She eyed the ride with suspicion. It was a bilious shade of green and had eight long tentacles with seats attached at the ends. The tentacles were fastened to a tall thick pole. The object of the ride seemed to be to give the riders whiplash as it spun and twisted.

She wasn't terribly comfortable with them going, but they were so excited she found she couldn't say no. As they got to the top of the stairs, she remembered the tickets, and cut in behind them.

"Three?" the ride operator asked as he tore off the tickets.

Zack and C.J. had raced ahead and were already climbing into their seats.

"No." She motioned at the boys. "Just those two."

"Lady," he said, obviously annoyed, "they aren't tall enough to ride by themselves. You have to go along."

She shook her head. She hated rides like this. But she hated to disappoint her son. How bad could the ride be? She'd done so much in the past week she hadn't realized she could do. Heck, she thought with a grin, she'd made love in a jail cell. Why not ride the Octopus? Take a chance, she told herself.

Palms sweating, she stepped up and buckled herself in beside Zack. The look of utter excitement on his face calmed her down. It would last only a few minutes.

How bad could it be?

Trace had been looking for Jenn. He spotted her in the distance on the platform of the Octopus. He'd stopped by the barn to check on Kelly's readiness for the judging tomorrow and she'd told him Jenn was here.

He needed to see her again. Tonight, if possible.

He knew she was busy now that Miranda was home from the hospital, but maybe he'd sneak her away for a late dinner, a nice romantic meal, just the two of them.

Just thinking about the other night brought a grin to his face. He'd hoped at some point Jenn would be willing, but when she'd kissed him back as if she'd meant business, the smoldering feelings he'd had for her since she'd come back to Blossom had burst into flame and consumed them both.

She'd certainly let herself go, he remembered, his body growing warm and heavy with the familiar ache that had been plaguing him ever since she'd returned.

It had been a memorable evening.

He'd never feel the same about cell number four again.

He grinned. Might have to get a plaque and put it up on the wall above the door. He pondered the wording as he got to the base of the ride.

The Octopus started up slowly with a loud grinding noise. It sounded as if it needed grease, he thought as watched Jenn's hands clutch the handle bar, her knuckles white. Her face was set in an expression of grim resolve, and her lips were pressed together in a grimace. She looked like a woman enduring torture, and the ride was barely moving.

He waved as they went by on the first rotation. Zack waved back, but Jenn had her eyes closed. Her son looked as if he was in heaven. Trace wished he was up there with them. He loved the feeling of speed and movement on the carnival rides. From the look on Zack's face, he could see the little boy felt the same.

As the ride spun, tentacles flung the riders up and then down as well as around. Trace moved toward the exit stairs on the far side of the platform. The squeals and screams from the riders increased with the speed. He wanted to be right there when Jenn walked off. Curiosity had him wanting to find out why she'd gone on the ride.

The ride seemed to be going faster than it normally did, but that was probably because he was standing closer than usual. At this position, he couldn't see the riders' faces, just their feet and legs. He recognized Jenn's shapely tan calves and ankles as they flew by.

Just as it registered with him that the ride was indeed running at a higher speed than normal, the ride's operator starting yelling and sparks began shooting from the gearbox at the base of the pole under the platform.

Heart pounding with fear, Trace raced to the operator, who was punching buttons on the control panel with his fist and swearing. Jenn's white face went by in a flash, her eyes huge with terror. The woman he loved was on that ride, and the thought of her being in danger hit him like a blow to his gut.

The operator, who had hurtled down the stairs and was now hunched under the platform, was trying to get close enough to the gearbox to reach the main power switch. Flames, sparks and small pieces of hot metal spewed from the mechanism, pinging off the base of the ride. With an oath, the man jerked his arm back, his face clearly showing his fear of the sparks and flame.

Trace let out a roar of anger and frustration at the operator's reticence, grabbed the man's waistband and pulled him out of the way.

There was only one thing on his mind. Jenn was in danger. He needed to stop the ride before the vibration caused the thing to disintegrate.

He crawled closer on his belly and reached for the handle, ignoring the sting of the sparks. No amount of heat or fire was going to stop him from getting Jenn to safety. He yanked on the switch, and it wouldn't budge. The metal shaft with plastic handle, warped and twisted from the heat, was jammed in the open position. Smoke poured from the box, and the smell of burning insulation drifted in the air.

"Where's the power source?" Trace yelled.

The frightened operator blinked twice, then stuttered and pointed. "B-back here."

Trace climbed over the cables like a crab. He could feel the heat coming off the ride, and the increased shuddering threatened to shake the platform loose above his head. With resolute determination he grabbed the overheated power box.

The industrial-sized plug apparatus was held into the metal housing with several wraps of duct tape. Trace tore at the tape as the vibration increased.

Over the noise he yelled, "Get out there and move people away from the ride."

The man stared at him for a moment as if he didn't understand.

"Now, go!" Trace yelled, and gave him a shove.

As he scooted out from under the ride, Trace could hear him yelling at the crowd to get back.

Trace fought to unwrap the tape from the plug, tearing at it with his teeth. He finally worked off enough of the tape to rip the plug out of the housing. The motor went dead, but the platform continued to shudder as the rotations of the arms slowed.

Trace scrambled out from under the ride as the Octopus came to a jerky stop. He took the stairs three at a time. Smoke still poured from the motor, rising up through the holes in the metal platform like some spooky Halloween special effect.

For an instant everything was quiet, then the riders began scrambling out of their seats and off the platform.

Jenn was on the far side of the ride, and Trace made his way around to her. Zack and C.J. were already out of their seats, but Jenn was fumbling with her own belt, her hands shaking so badly she couldn't seem to manage. The three of them looked pale and frightened.

"You boys okay?" He took his eyes off Jenn long enough to speak directly to Zack.

Two little heads nodded in unison.

He turned them around and gave them a gentle

push. "I'll get your mom. Wait at the bottom of the stairs."

Holding hands, the boys scrambled down the steps.

Trace and Jenn were the last ones left on the platform. He brushed her trembling hands aside, his own not much steadier. "Let me do that."

As he opened the catch on her harness tears welled in her eyes.

"I was so scared," she said in a tiny, quavering voice.

He put his hands under her arms and helped her to her feet, then pulled her against his body. Her arms went around his waist and she clutched the back of his shirt.

"So was I. So was I," he said into her hair as he held her shaking body.

The platform swayed and listed to the left, and Jenn gasped into the front of his shirt.

"Can you walk?" he asked. They needed to get down on solid ground. Now.

She nodded, but clung to him as he guided her down the steps. "What happened?"

"I don't know, but I'm sure going to find out." With the help of one of the head carnival workers, Carlo Fuentes, Trace had inspected all the rides before the fair opened, and none had had tape around the housing for the power source.

When they were on solid ground Trace allowed himself a sigh of relief. They reached Zack and the two boys nestled against her side.

Trace wanted to hold her like this and keep her safe.

Forever.

It seemed so simple and clear to him. They belonged together. He didn't care if they lived in Blossom or Dallas, as long as they were together.

He spotted Carlo Fuentes striding toward them.

"Fuentes. We've got a problem," he said, his voice sharp.

Carlo nodded and tipped his head toward Jenn. "Everyone okay?"

Trace said, "Shaken, but no one appears injured."

"Except you." He indicated Trace's arms and hands.

Trace looked down, surprised to see his sleeve was singed and his skin blistered and black in spots.

Jenn made a sound of concern, then took both his hands and examined his burned skin.

The ride's operator walked up and Fuentes turned to him. "What happened?"

The man shrugged and stuffed his hands into his pockets, his shoulders moving up and down in a jerking motion. "Malfunction?"

Trace took a step toward Fuentes. "That was no malfunction. Take a look at the power source. We've got a case of sabotage here."

Carlo's features hardened. "You sure?"

Trace watched the man carefully, his mind sorting out all the details of the incident. "Not a doubt in my mind. You have enemies, Fuentes?" he asked, curious how the man would respond.

Fuentes narrowed his eyes, but didn't look away. "Apparently."

Good answer, Trace thought. He had expected an outright denial of any problems, or claims that the mishap was an accident. It didn't matter what Fuentes thought. Trace would find whoever had done this and they would pay. He'd investigate and see that the person responsible served time.

He nodded at Fuentes. "Rope off the area and keep everyone out. I'll be back to investigate this."

The carny nodded and turned toward the ride.

The muscle in Trace's cheek clenched. No one put the woman he loved in danger without answering to him.

His feelings had nothing to do with being sheriff.

Jenn was his. She always had been and she always would be. That had become clear to him the other night, and today had convinced him beyond any doubt.

He drew Jenn to his side. "Come on, I'll drive you home."

"I'm okay to drive. You need to have your burns treated."

He didn't want her to drive. She was still too shaky. "I'll drop you off and then I'll go." She was right. Now that the excitement was over, his hands and arms were starting to throb.

She nodded, and let him lead her to his car. The little boys followed along.

C.J. stopped and gaped at the cruiser. "Do we get to ride in the police car?" he asked, his eyes as big as saucers.

"Sure do." Trace opened the back door and both boys scrambled in.

Jenn directed him to C.J.'s house, then got out with the boys and walked them into the house. While she was inside, Trace called Henrie to tell her to send a deputy to the fairgrounds to secure the area around the Octopus. His dispatcher already knew the entire story. You had to love a small town, he thought.

Jenn came out of the house alone, and walked toward him in the bright sunlight.

He'd never seen a more beautiful sight in his life.

How was he going to convince her to stay? What words could he use? This would be the most important speech he ever made.

She slid into the passenger seat.

"Zack?" he asked, wondering if her son was coming.

She shook her head and smiled. "He's going to stay with C.J. They're busy telling their adventure to C.J.'s older brothers."

"Is his mom upset?" he asked. "I could go in and talk to her."

Jenn laughed, and the sound made his heart swell. She seemed to be recovering from her scare.

"She took it in stride. C.J. is the youngest of five boys. Maybe you don't worry so much with your fifth." She gave a shaky laugh.

He reached across the seat and squeezed her hand. "She wasn't there to watch it happen. It scared the hell out of me."

She looked at him, a surprised expression on her face. "You seemed so, I don't know, cool and in charge."

He blew out an unsteady breath and hooked his arm around her shoulders, pulling her across the seat. "Oh, babe, I've never been so scared," he said.

She clung to him for a moment, then broke away and fastened her seat belt. "Now we go and get you taken care of."

"I can drop you off at home. I know how you feel about the hospital."

"I'm going with you," she said in a determined voice.

Trace wasn't going to argue. They drove in silence. Jenn stared out the window, and he watched her out of the corner of his eye, mentally cataloguing all the reasons she should stay in Blossom. He'd start his campaign to keep her here as soon as he got medical care. His hands and arms were throbbing, but he figured the injuries looked worse than they were.

"Wait and I'll get your door," she said once they reached the hospital.

He was too tired to argue, so he let her fuss over him. It would take her mind off the scare she'd had. As soon as he washed off the soot and grime, his burns would be okay.

The waiting room was empty and the screening nurse led them through a set of swinging doors to an exam room. "The doctor's setting a broken bone, so it will be a few minutes." She opened a cupboard and took out a gown. "Take off your shirt and put this on."

Jenn took the gown from the nurse.

The nurse pulled the curtain closed and said, "I'll tell him you're here." Her voice faded as the door closed.

Trace was having trouble with his shirt. His fingertips were blistered and sore. Jenn brushed his hands aside and stood in front of him to unbutton his shirt. He propped his forearms on her shoulders and leaned down to nuzzle her neck.

She laughed and jerked to the side, trying to avoid his mouth. "Trace! For heaven's sake!"

It was good to hear her laugh. "What's the matter, Jenn?" He planted a kiss on her cheek just beside her lips.

"The doctor could come in any minute!"

He enjoyed the bloom of color on her cheeks as she slid his shirt down his arms and gently pulled it past his injured hands. She unfolded the cotton gown and held it up so he could slip his hands through the armholes, then she carefully eased the gown up his arms, trying to avoid scraping the material over his burns. She made sympathetic noises and murmured over his injuries as if he were a child. He loved every second of her attention.

He knew he should wait until another time, take her out to a special restaurant, a romantic dinner, but he couldn't wait. Today had pointed out to him in the most graphic way that life could change in a heartbeat.

He put his arms over her shoulders again before she could back away. He wanted to hold her, but the pain was blooming in his injured skin and his arms were smeared with dirt and soot.

He cleared his throat. "Jenn, I want you to stay."

She nodded. "I will, if it's okay with the doctor."

"No. I mean I want you to stay with me. I don't want you to get the annulment. I want us to be married."

At first she looked surprised, then frightened. She opened her mouth, then didn't seem to know what to say. Her jaw snapped shut and she looked down at her feet. "Trace, I…"

He put his singed index finger under her chin and tipped her head up so he could see her face. He wasn't going to give her a chance to say no. Not this time. "I love you, Jenn. I always have and I always will."

Her eyes teared up and she shook her head. "My life is in Dallas. And yours is here."

He loved her too much to have geography stand in their way. He wasn't going to let where they lived be an obstacle.

Trace said, "I'll go to Dallas to be with you."

She gave him a sad smile. "You'd hate living in the city."

She hadn't moved an inch, but he could feel her pulling away. Quietly he said, "I'd do it for you. I'd do anything for you."

There was a brisk knock on the door. She jerked away from him.

Damn, he thought, the doctor's timing sucked. Trace said, "Come in" in a curt voice.

Jenn took a seat in the chair in the corner as the

doctor pushed the curtain aside. He introduced himself and examined Trace's hands and arms.

"You're going to need to have these cleaned out. I'll see if the operating room is available."

Trace had been half listening as he thought about what he was going to say to Jenn to convince her to marry him. The doctor's words sank in.

"Operating room? Can't you just do it in here?" He needed to finish his conversation with Jenn.

The doctor shook his head and frowned. "Some of these burns are deep, and they all need to be cleaned out. It's more than I can do under a local anesthetic." He pushed an intercom button by the door and asked the nurse to bring in a wheelchair.

"But—"

Jenn's voice cut him off. "Trace."

"What?" he said more sharply than he had intended. She walked to his side and rubbed his shoulder.

He felt like a heel for snapping at her. "Sorry."

"Do what the doctor says. We can talk later."

Trace closed his eyes and sighed as he nodded. What else could he do? Why did life always seem to conspire against him and Jenn? It should be easy. He loved her and he knew she loved him.

She reached up and kissed him on the cheek. "I'll take you home. We can talk tonight," she said, then scooted out the door.

"Jenn, wait." She didn't come back.

He didn't want Jenn to have all afternoon to stew over what he'd said.

"Tonight!" he called after her as the nurse opened the door and wheeled in the chair.

Tonight he'd make her understand how much she meant to him.

Tonight he'd convince her they belonged together.

Dallas or Blossom, he thought as he lowered himself into the wheelchair. It didn't matter, as long as they were together.

Chapter Sixteen

Jenn sat in the hospital waiting room and thought about Trace's proposal.

He'd said he'd always loved her and he always would.

After the past few weeks, she knew she felt the same. But was it enough?

They'd fallen in love as little more than children, and since she'd come back they'd had a summer fling. Did they have the kind of love it would take to build a life together? There were so many things to consider.

She liked her life in Dallas just the way it was. She had Zack and her job. She'd worked hard to arrange her life to suit her. Did she want to upset all their lives by having him move to Dallas?

She'd been serious when she'd told him he'd hate it. Trace belonged in Blossom. He loved the outdoors; hunting and fishing on his days off were his greatest joy.

He had stature as sheriff. What would he do in Dallas? Join the police force and be a street cop? He'd be happier and safer in Blossom.

She looked down and realized she was in the process of shredding her thumbnail.

All her reservations were valid, but she needed to face her worst fear.

What if she said yes to Trace, and he moved to Dallas. What if it didn't work out for them? Could her heart take the pain?

She didn't think it could.

"Jennifer?" The nurse's voice interrupted her dismal thoughts.

"Yes?"

"Trace is ready to go."

"Thanks." Now they would have to talk, she thought, wishing she'd had more time to think things over.

The nurse handed her a printed list of instructions on changing bandages, and a white sack. "Here's his medication and ointment. His follow-up appointment is written on the top of the sheet." She dropped Trace's keys into Jenn's hand. "He can't drive. Better you should have these so he doesn't try."

She looked down at the keys. "Why not?"

"He's had a lot of pain medication. You bring the car around to the entrance, and I'll wheel him out." She turned on her squeaky rubber shoes and disappeared.

By the time she pulled up in the car, Trace was out front. He had his eyes closed and was listing to one side. His arms and hands were heavily bandaged.

Her eyes teared up. Did he have any idea how brave he was? She knew he'd shrug off any praise she could come up with.

"Hey, babe. Missed you," he said when he spotted her, his words slurred and his grin crooked.

He grabbed her hand and tried to pull her down onto his lap with his bandaged hands.

"Whoa, tiger," the nurse said, laughing. "Save it for later."

Jenn felt her face heat. "I see what you mean about driving." She stepped back as he made another grab for her, and let the nurse guide him into the car.

By the time they left the parking lot, Trace was asleep.

She had to shake him awake at his house and guide him to his bedroom. He sat on the side of the bed in a stupor and let her undress him. When he flopped back on the bed and started to snore, she had to admit she was relieved.

Their talk would wait. It would give her time to think.

Jenn waited at the entrance to the carousel where she'd agreed to meet Trace and Zack.

She and Trace hadn't talked yet. The past two days had been full of activity, with the 4H judging and Trace catching up on work he'd missed. Between

Zack and Kelly and Miranda and the baby there had been constant interruptions.

This morning Trace had taken Zack out to the Tucker place for another riding lesson while she'd worked in the conference room on the land swindle. It was tedious, but she loved it. It was like fitting together a giant puzzle, getting all the pieces in the right places so she could see the whole picture.

She was close to figuring it out.

"Have you found what you thought was lost?" a soft, familiar voice said from behind her.

Jenn turned. Cherry, the fortune-teller, stepped up to stand beside her. She was dressed in a swirling skirt of vibrant colors, and a matching scarf held back her wild, curly hair.

"I, uh, I'm not sure." The woman had taken her by surprise.

She patted Jenn on the arm. "You will be sure. Just listen to your heart." She smiled and walked off into the crowd.

Bemused, Jenn watched her go, wondering about the odd follow-up to the reading.

Jenn turned her attention back to the whirling carousel. Kelly was going to join them for lunch, and undoubtedly Ryan would arrive with her niece. She scanned the crowd. Then she glanced at her watch. Part of her worried about Zack riding on a horse, though she trusted Trace completely.

The thought caused her to catch her breath. She *did* trust him, and in all these years, that had never changed. He was as steady as a rock, and as dependable as the sunrise.

The music stopped and the gates opened, letting the riders out. An adorable little girl standing next to her was vibrating with excitement.

She caught Jenn's eye, and asked, "What color horse do you want?"

Jenn smiled down at her. "I'm not going to ride."

The little girl's eyes widened with amazement. "Why not?"

Jenn shrugged. Why not? She looked around again and couldn't see Trace.

Why not take a ride? She'd always loved the carousel. It was certainly more her speed than the Octopus. She shuddered at the memory of that wild ride.

She smiled at the child again. "On second thought, I think I will go. What horse do you want?"

Without hesitation the child answered, "Oh, the white one with the golden tail."

Jenn knew the horse. As a child it had been her favorite, too, with its garland of carved pink roses along the saddle.

"I think I'll ride the black one." She pulled money out of her pocket and handed it to the attendant for her ticket as she moved along with the crowd of excited children.

She found the sleek black horse, carved with its front and back legs extended as if in full gallop, and climbed aboard. Slowly the music started and Jenn's horse began its gentle up-and-down movement. Lights flashed as they reflected off the mirrors mounted on the gaily painted center of the merry-go-round. As the ride picked up speed, with every revolution Jenn kept her eye on the entrance, watching for Trace and Zack.

Suddenly they were there. A lump formed in her throat as she went around and around, catching their images for a split second with each turn. Trace had made such an effort with Zack, and it truly touched her. He was such a hero, in so many ways.

The next time he came into view, Kelly was standing there, and right behind her was Ryan. Her niece looked happier than Jenn had seen her all summer. Two more times around, and she was surprised to see Miranda there with the baby in a stroller. Kelly must have told her mom where they were meeting.

As the merry-go-round continued to spin, a thought hit her.

Everyone she loved was right there, waiting for her.

She loved Trace. She'd fallen for him when she was fourteen and she knew without a doubt she'd love him until the day she died. Tears gathered at the back of her throat and she felt her eyes sting. Why had it taken her so long to see that what she wanted and needed was right here, in Blossom?

Suddenly she knew what the fortune-teller had meant. She had lost something.

She had a house and job in Dallas, but her heart was in Blossom. That was what she had needed to find. She had needed to come home. Home to Blossom.

She wiped at her eyes, and then heard the excited squeal of the riders and the unmistakable ching of the brass rings sliding down the chute. She reached up and hooked one of the thick rings as she went by, closing her fist around it and bringing her hand up to her heart.

A while ago she'd wondered if there was any feeling better than falling in love for the first time. Now she had her answer. It was falling in love for the last time.

This was where she belonged, right here in Blossom.

The ride began to slow and she caught Trace's eye. He tapped Zack on the shoulder and pointed to her as she went by the next time.

She held up the brass ring, and he grinned.

The ride came to a halt and the attendant walked by and traded her brass ring for another ticket.

She pocketed the ticket and walked off the ride. Trace met her at the gate. "Brass ring? Must be your lucky day."

She grabbed his hand and Zack's and towed them both back to the carousel. "You don't know how right you are!" she said, and laughed as the music started up again.

Jenn laid out a blanket on the grass, as far as possible from the other people who had gathered for the fireworks. She set the picnic basket on the corner of the blanket. Along with fried chicken she'd brought champagne and strawberries and crystal glasses.

She looked at her watch. Trace had promised he would be here when he finished his shift. Nervously she smoothed the blanket and checked the contents of the basket.

It was one of those perfect summer nights. The air was warm and the sky was clear and a huge full moon had just risen over the horizon.

What would he say, she wondered? He'd been hurt by her refusals. Had he had time to reconsider? Maybe when she proposed he'd decide it wasn't a good idea after all.

Stop being such a ninny, she chided herself.

He'd say yes.

He had to say yes.

She felt as if her life depended on it.

She glanced at her watch again. He should be here by now. She smoothed the blanket again and arranged the full skirt of her sundress.

How did you propose to someone you were already married to? Did they have to get married again? She remembered little of the hasty ceremony in New Mexico. She'd been so young and scared.

He arrived with the first burst of explosions. He stood by the blanket, his head and torso backlit by a burst of green and blue sparks.

"Hey, Jenn." His soft familiar greeting caused flutter in her midsection. He dropped onto the blanket, then immediately hooked his arm around her waist and hauled her up against him for a kiss.

A rocket shrieked into the sky, exploding into dozens of golden showers as he worked his magic on her mouth.

When he had her breathless, he pulled back and looked at her. "I've been thinking about that all day." He grinned, his teeth looking very white in the darkness.

She hauled him back for another kiss. "So have I."

She turned to the basket. "Hungry?" she asked, and then yelped when he grabbed her ankle, pulled her down and pinned her with his big warm body.

His hand smoothed up her bare leg where her skirt had ridden up and he bit at her ear. "Starving."

She tried to scramble up, but he was lying on her skirt. "Trace! There are people around."

He gave her a wicked smile as she yanked on her skirt, finally freeing it. "So?"

"So you need to show some decorum, Sheriff." She laughed and turned back to the basket.

His warm hand wrapped around her ankle again. "I find that hard to do when I'm with you."

She looked back over her shoulder, loving the fact that she had that effect on him. "Chicken?"

"It's a poor second to what I want, but okay."

Jenn handed him a piece. "You took off the big bandages."

"Doc did. He says I'm healing well," he said around a bite of chicken.

She was far too nervous to eat, so she split her time between watching the fireworks and Trace.

He finished his chicken and reached for her again, pulling her down with him and nestling her against his side as they both lay on their backs.

He reached up and smoothed her hair. "Remember the last time we did this?"

She kissed the side of his face. "Oh, yes." Eight years ago, the day before she realized she was pregnant. She'd never forget that night. "Seems like a long time," she murmured.

"Sometimes it seems like yesterday." He squeezed her hand.

They watched the finale, then lay there together as the lights in the parking lot came on and everyone around them got up and started moving toward their cars.

Trace turned and nipped at her ear. "You keeping me here until everyone leaves so you can have your way with me?"

She shook her head. "I need to talk to you."

"What's wrong?" He went very still beside her.

She raised herself up on one elbow so she could see his face. "Today, on the merry-go-round, I realized something. I was watching you and Zack and Miranda and her children as I went by, and it hit me. Everything I love is here in Blossom."

At first he didn't say anything, and she bit back a wave of nerves.

He tucked her hair behind her ear. "What are you going to do about it?"

She smiled at him. "Well, I was planning to propose to you, but we're still married. So I'm not sure what to ask you."

He enfolded her in his arms and held her against

his chest, where she could feel the comforting steady beat of his heart.

"Ah, Jenn, you make my heart sing."

How had she ever thought she could go back to Dallas and live without this man?

He rolled a little to the side and dug in his pocket, then picked up her left hand and slid a ring onto her third finger. "You say you're not sure what to ask me? How about if you ask me if I'll love you and take care of you for the rest of my life?"

"That works for me." She glanced at the simple gold ring he'd placed on her finger, then she pulled him back into her arms and held on, feeling a gentle peace settle over her.

She was home.

Forever.

* * * * *

Don't miss the finale of
BLOSSOM COUNTY FAIR.
Where love blooms true!

HER GYPSY PRINCE
by Crystal Green
Silhouette Romance #1789
October 2005

SILHOUETTE *Romance*®

Don't miss the final moments of the

Blossom County *Fair*

Where love blooms true!

To sheltered debutante Elizabeth Dupres, Carlo Fuentes looked like a swashbuckling pirate—handsome, debonair… a man a good girl like her shouldn't want. But she did. And for the first time in her life, Elizabeth just might be willing to risk everything she'd ever been for the woman she could become in his arms….

Her Gypsy Prince
(SR #1789)

by CRYSTAL GREEN
Available October 2005

Only from Silhouette Books!

Visit Silhouette Books at www.eHarlequin.com

SRHGP

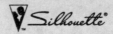

SPECIAL EDITION™

Go on an emotional journey in

JOAN ELLIOTT PICKART's

new romance

HOME AGAIN

Available September 2005
Silhouette Special Edition #1705

Convinced that her infertility would destroy any relationship, psychologist Cedar Kennedy vowed never to fall in love again. But when dream-come-true Mark Chandler stole her heart and offered her a future, Cedar was torn between the promise of their love…and fear she'll never have a happy home.

Available at your favorite retail outlet.

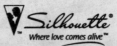

Where love comes alive™

Visit Silhouette Books at www.eHarlequin.com   SSEHA

This September,

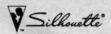

‑ S P E C I A L E D I T I O N ™ ‑

brings you the third book in
the exciting new continuity

Eleven students.
One reunion.
And a secret that will
change everyone's lives.

THE MEASURE OF A MAN
(SE #1706)

by award-winning author

MARIE FERRARELLA

Jane Johnson had worked at her alma mater for several
years before the investigation into her boss, Professor
Gilbert Harrison, put her job at risk. Desperate to keep her
income, Jane begged her former classmate Smith Parker
to help her find secret information that could exonerate
the professor. Smith was reluctant—he wanted to stay
out of trouble—but he couldn't resist the charms of the
beautiful single mom. The hours they spent together soon
led to intense sparks…and all-out passion. But when an
old secret threatens Smith's job—and his reputation—will
the fallout put an end to their happiness forever?

*Don't miss this compelling story—
only from Silhouette Books.*

Available at your favorite retail outlet.

Visit Silhouette Books at www.eHarlequin.com   SSETMOAM

If you enjoyed what you just read,
then we've got an offer you can't resist!

Take 2 bestselling love stories FREE!

Plus get a FREE surprise gift!

Clip this page and mail it to Silhouette Reader Service™

IN U.S.A.	IN CANADA
3010 Walden Ave.	P.O. Box 609
P.O. Box 1867	Fort Erie, Ontario
Buffalo, N.Y. 14240-1867	L2A 5X3

YES! Please send me 2 free Silhouette Romance® novels and my free surprise gift. After receiving them, if I don't wish to receive anymore, I can return the shipping statement marked cancel. If I don't cancel, I will receive 4 brand-new novels every month, before they're available in stores! In the U.S.A., bill me at the bargain price of $3.57 plus 25¢ shipping and handling per book and applicable sales tax, if any*. In Canada, bill me at the bargain price of $4.05 plus 25¢ shipping and handling per book and applicable taxes**. That's the complete price and a savings of at least 10% off the cover prices—what a great deal! I understand that accepting the 2 free books and gift places me under no obligation ever to buy any books. I can always return a shipment and cancel at any time. Even if I never buy another book from Silhouette, the 2 free books and gift are mine to keep forever.

210 SDN DZ7L
310 SDN DZ7M

Name   (PLEASE PRINT)

Address   Apt.#

City   State/Prov.   Zip/Postal Code

Not valid to current Silhouette Romance® subscribers.

Want to try two free books from another series?
Call 1-800-873-8635 or visit www.morefreebooks.com.

* Terms and prices subject to change without notice. Sales tax applicable in N.Y.
** Canadian residents will be charged applicable provincial taxes and GST.
All orders subject to approval. Offer limited to one per household.
® are registered trademarks owned and used by the trademark owner and or its licensee.

SROM04R   ©2004 Harlequin Enterprises Limited

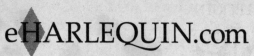

eHARLEQUIN.com

The Ultimate Destination for Women's Fiction

Visit eHarlequin.com's Bookstore today
for today's most popular books at great prices.

- An extensive selection of romance books by top authors!

- Choose our convenient "bill me" option. No credit card required.

- New releases, Themed Collections and hard-to-find backlist.

- A sneak peek at upcoming books.

- Check out book excerpts, book summaries and Reader Recommendations from other members and post your own too.

- Find out what everybody's reading in Bestsellers.

- Save BIG with everyday discounts and exclusive online offers!

- Our Category Legend will help you select reading that's exactly right for you!

- Visit our Bargain Outlet often for huge savings and special offers!

- Sweepstakes offers. Enter for your chance to win special prizes, autographed books and more.

Your purchases are 100% guaranteed—so shop online at www.eHarlequin.com today!

INTBB104R

HARLEQUIN®

Looking forward to your NEXT™ novel?

Coming in September:

Four new titles are available each month!

Every Life Has More Than One Chapter™

Available wherever Harlequin books are sold.

www.TheNextNovel.com
HNSEPGEN